Maid for Me

Written by Kat Lieu

ISBN-13: 978-0-9821881-1-8

DEDICATION

Maid for Me began in 2007 on fictionpress.com and has had a huge fan following since its inception. I want to thank all my readers, supporters, fans, and my beloved Nummyz.com forum moderators. You've been through thick and thin with me. You've followed me through junior high, to high school, to college. I love you gals and guys! ☺

Written by Kat Lieu
Copyright 2010 by Kat Lieu, all rights reserved.
Cover art by Eve Lieu, mayuiki.deviantart.com

ISBN-13: 978-0-9821881-1-8

~*~

This is a work of fiction. Names, characters, places and incidents are either the product of the author's imagination or used fictitiously and any resemblance to actual persons, living or dead, business establishments, events or locales is entirely coincidental.

ONE

"Mouuusssee-cake..."

One block away from Bubble Café, Mina Lin's mouth flooded with drool. She licked her lips, dreaming about the amazing green-tea mousse cake her best friend had reserved for her. The cake was so special. This was because pâtissier only made it fresh once a month. The birthday version of the cake was two-tiered, layered with mint cream, and filled with melt-on-your-tongue matcha-mousse.

Usually, birthdays were like any other day to Mina. This year though, she had looked forward to her birthday for at least six weeks.

It wasn't because it was her sweet-sixteenth birthday. It was because Mina was sure Kiterin Forrests, her best and only boy friend, would confess his love for her as the ultimate birthday gift.

Okay... Maybe not. I'm the one confessing today.

Five summers ago, Mina had seen Kit shirtless while mowing the lawn next door. Sweat made his sun-kissed boy- pecs glisten. He wiped his forehead with the back of his hand, sweeping away his wheat-colored bangs. Mina had wanted to give her new neighbor a towel, and then keep the towel after he was done using it, just as a stalker would. When Kit noticed Mina, he blinked his ivy-colored eyes and smiled directly at her.

Instead of smiling back, Mina ran into her house and wondered if her pounding heart would pop out of her chest.

1

That wasn't the exact moment she had fallen in love with Kit though. A week later, Mina's father had a stroke at work. He had died in the hospital emergency room before Mina and her mother had a chance to see him one last time.

Kit and his parents had attended the funeral. That day, Mina stayed at the graveyard until nightfall, alone. Leaving, she stumbled over a tombstone and fell into an open grave. At first, she screamed and cried. Minutes later, when no one came to her rescue, she just lay there, waiting to be buried and thinking she would see her daddy soon.

Kit, who had stayed behind, had found Mina. He pulled her out of the grave and brought her home. The next day, he read her a poem he had written when his grandmother passed away. Reciting the poem, beautiful tears ran down his cheeks.

That was the exact moment Mina had fallen in love with Kit.

Ever since then, Kit had stayed by Mina's side like as if he was a guardian angel. On special occasions, he surprised her with hand-made gifts such as sculpted and whittled duck figurines. He even traveled with her to and from school on a daily basis.

Was it any surprise she was so obsessed with Kit?

For the past five years, even though Mina had kept her feelings for her best friend a secret, everyone and their grannies could see how much she loved him.

Everyone except for Kit, that was. Mina had always wondered why he was so oblivious to her feelings. He usually had more sensitivity in his left pinky than most guys had in their entire bodies.

When they read Romeo and Juliet together in the eighth grade, Kit wept during the part the star-crossed lovers died. Mina, on the other hand, thought the entire tragedy could have been avoided if Romeo had a smartphone.

Snapping Mina out of her thoughts, Kit asked, "Aren't you excited?" His voice was deep and lyrical like an aria to her ears. He walked behind Mina at a sloth's pace. Unlike other Uptowners, Kit's motto was "stop and smell the roses."

In the summer, the Uptown was muggy enough to annoy mosquitoes. Everyone who had AC blasted their units, leading to frequent citywide blackouts.

Crankiness-levels rose like the temperature. Even on the weekends, people roamed the streets like they were high on Red Bull and caffeine. Drivers honked at anyone or anything that didn't move quickly enough, like shaky, little old ladies crossing the streets with their rolling walkers. Or like Kit.

Trying to be more like Kit, Mina forced herself to relax and smell roses-whenever she could find roses in the city at least. She looked down and studied their shadows. Kit's shadow and hers melded together.

Like we're one.

Her heart skipped a beat. She spun around, her cheeks flushed and glowing. She loved the way Kit dressed- today he wore a white t-shirt, faded blue jeans and black flip-flops. Everything about Kit was adorable to Mina, even his toes.

"Very excited," she replied and clapped, trying to look adorable. Turning around again, she tripped on a crack and almost launched herself down the busy city street. Arms flailing, she regained her balance and avoided a face-first-fiasco on the ground.

I can't afford to be so clumsy if I didn't have such good reflexes.

Her ears burned when Kit and other pedestrians laughed. She scrambled to straighten herself.

That's the last time I'm trying to look cute, she told herself firmly.

"You okay?" Kit asked, grinning. Mina smiled and nodded before continuing to walk, stopping to think about how she was walking, trying to maneuver just as a robot would: on two feet.

"You're really something else," Kit muttered.

"Yea, thanks." Mina chuckled, taking his comment as a compliment. As much as she tried, she didn't know the definition of flirting or acting girly. She liked martial arts, action films, and dressing like a tomboy to hide her baby-fat. Her outfit would often consist of what she wore now, a loose black t-shirt, khaki boy shorts, and worn white sneakers.

Her embarrassment faded as she inhaled the smoggy city air and smiled. She wouldn't want to spend this beautiful and toasty Saturday afternoon any other way.

To celebrate her birthday, Kit had taken the day off from his summer job at LAG, a prestigious art institute. He had promised Mina he would spend the entire day with her.

If that's not love, then I don't know what is, she thought happily to herself

Kit had spent all semester trying to perfect his LAG application, just so the institute would consider him since they usually preferred hiring college students. His dream was to become an art professor.

Working at LAG would give him a taste of the career he wished to pursue.

Mina could see it now. After wolfing down delicious cake, she would confess her feelings to Kit. Then they would date, get married, and have a happily ever after together like characters in fairytales. The Wedding March tune played in her head. She could see a litter of their chubby children running around their future home-a house Mina would build.

Okay, so maybe I should just focus on senior prom first.

Kit's shadow separated from Mina's when they made a turn at the street corner.

A minute later, they arrived in front of Bubble Café and entered through blue glass doors. Young people filled the inside, giving it a high school cafeteria feel. Mina loved Bubble Café's design-the blue and green polka-dotted exterior and interior, the navy-blue plastic bubble seats, and light-cerulean circular tables. A mixture of fragrant scents from aromatic coffee and sweets greeted her nose. Mina wondered if she could get diabetes from just inhaling all the sugary sweetness.

"You know, the owners of this place are lovers," Kit said.

"Really?" Mina's cheeks grew warm. *Is he implying something?*

Kit led her toward a table in the center of the café.

Mina frowned when she noticed a girl at their table. Hesitating to sit, Mina recognized the girl.

Why is Alyssa Rabinkaya, otherwise known as Miss Bimbo Cheerleader and Ultimate Popularity at Uptown High, here?

Her impressive stats: 34-C, 22, 36 versus Mina's 32A/B, 32, 32. Alyssa had Godiva's long blond locks, pore-less tanned skin, and large, expressive gray eyes. In a fantasy world, Alyssa would be a woodland nymph and Mina would be a hairy gnome.

Mina wiped her sweaty neck with a tissue, leaving white paper-bits on her skin. Kit took a seat next to Alyssa. Not telling Mina to sit, he acted as if he had already forgotten that his best friend existed.

Mina felt a sharp pang in her chest, like someone had just stabbed her heart with a poisoned dagger.

Doomsday, doomsday, doomsday, were the words echoing in her head.

Half of the girls at Uptown High, including Alyssa, admired Kit. In school, he was popular because he often won citywide painting contests. Every month, the school lobby featured one of his award-winning paintings.

Mina didn't care about the other girls; Kit didn't acknowledge their existence. Alyssa, however, was a class-A threat, since Kit seemed to pay her special attention.

Mina clenched her fists together. *I shouldn't be so paranoid, I mean... If Kit doesn't like me, then why would he spend so much time with me? Why would he be so considerate and nice to me? He knows everything about me and we've always been so close... I shouldn't be worried. Alyssa is just his new friend... not my love rival.*

Mina forced herself to breathe. *In like you're smelling roses, out like you're blowing out candles.*

Calm down and embrace Kit's new friend. Maybe you'll become good friends with her too!

"Alyssa?" Mina scratched her head. "What are you doing here?" Her voice cracked. She sat across from Alyssa and became stiff. Though they shared many classes together, Mina doubted Alyssa even knew her name.

Alyssa smiled. Her teeth were whiter than vanilla ice cream. "Kit invited me to celebrate your birthday, Mary."

I knew it! Do I even look like a Mary? I hate her already.

"Kit always talks about how great it would be for you to make more friends." Alyssa beamed at Kit and hugged her arm around his, leaning forward to give him a kiss on the cheek.

Mina's jaw dropped. The capillaries across Kit's face erupted. Mina didn't care if Alyssa called her Bob-the kiss she gave Kit made Mina want to rip out Alyssa's pretty blond hair and donate it to Locks of Love.

Still, before Mina could budge, five waiters dressed in the company's blue and white uniforms marched out of the kitchen. One carried the birthday cake-a big green creamy two-tiered cake with a dazzling sparkler atop it. Like a boy band, the men sang happy birthday to Alyssa. The waiter carrying the cake placed it down in front of her. Alyssa clapped, giggled, and blew out the sparkler. The waiters clapped too and winked at Alyssa before they disappeared back into the kitchen.

"Yay! Oops, I forgot-you should have blown out the candles, Mindy. I'll have the waiter light up the sparkler again." Alyssa snapped her fingers to summon a waiter. She leaned forward, her arms in front of her chest, squeezing her breasts together to make them look even fuller. One waiter materialized and all but drooled at the delectable sight of Alyssa.

Instead of adding a new sparkling atop the cake, the waiter kept drooling and bumped into another waiter carrying plates. The plates fell to the floor and Alyssa laughed, brushing hair away from her face.

Looking like that, she can probably command any straight male to do whatever she wishes. Even Kit is under her spell.

No... no... no.

Mina, giddy from denial, giggled like a ditz, just like Alyssa. She fanned her heated face. "I need some air."

Before Kit and Alyssa could see tears spill out of her eyes, Mina sprinted out of Bubble Café.

Outside in the bustling city street, Mina inhaled until her chest could expand no further. She shouted gibberish that rhymed with bit and tuck to release some steam. A minute passed. The second hand on Mina's one-dollar watch kept ticking and yet Kit remained inside the café.

Why isn't he coming out to see if I'm okay?

Mina had two options. She could run away. Or she could walk back into the café with her head held high and pretend she was fine. The latter would prove challenging-hiding her emotions was more difficult than passing advanced calculus. She wiped her wet eyes with the back of her hand.

It's either fight or flight and I always choose to fight!

Head held high, Mina strode back into the café with a weak smile plastered on her face.

"You okay, Min?" Kit asked, not looking into Mina's eyes.

"Yup." Whenever Mina lied, she looked at the floor and her nose twitched. This was something Kit had once pointed out.

"I'm fine." She sat down again.

Alyssa had already cut into the birthday cake and blurred out Mina's name with the knife. She held a fork in her hand and pretended it was an airplane flying toward Kit.

"Open wide, *pooki*," she said, feeding Kit the cake. Kit hesitated before he obliged, eating the cake with a big smile.

"So, you two are official?" Mina cut herself a slice of cake and stuffed it into her mouth.

Why does it taste so bitter? Must be too much matcha-powder.

Alyssa bobbed her head. "Kit asked me out last night. Yes,

we're officially boyfriend and girlfriend. Since you're Kit's best friend, you're the first to know." Alyssa beamed. "Kit says that I'm his inspiration and muse. Right, pooki?"

"Right, *mooki*." Kit grinned like a proud, unembarrassed boy-toy, still not looking at Mina. He didn't seem to mind the pet name calling either.

"By the way, I helped Kit choose this present for you. I hope you like it!" Alyssa handed Mina a thick pink envelope. Mina shook the envelope before she opened it.

"A gift card? Thanks." Mina squeezed the Trendy Star Fashion Boutique gift card so hard she was sure that it would break. Every size-zero female at school wore Trendy Star clothes. Was Kit trying to *transform* her into his dream girlfriend?

With her brows knitted, Mina slipped the card back into the envelope. Having expected something hand-made from Kit, the gift disappointed her. She had no words in her mental lexicon to describe her feeling right now.

"Nice clothes are very important, you know, *Meena*. If you're always dressed like a tomboy, it'll be very hard for you to find a boyfriend." Alyssa pouted. "And if you don't date in high school, it's very likely you'll be a spinster in the future."

Mina coughed. *Spinster? What are we, in the Eighteenth Century?*

"I like the way I dress," Mina replied, looking away from *Pooki* and *Mooki*.

"Kit had wanted to give you a whittled duckie or something silly like that, but that's so kiddie." Alyssa made a face.

Ducks were Mina's favorite animals. She loved her duckie-figurine collection. The duckies covered her nightstand in her bedroom. Every night before she slept, she played with them.

Mina stabbed her cake. If she had stabbed it any harder, she would have split the plate in two.

"Excuse me," Kit said. He hurried away from the table toward the restroom.

Mina sliced herself another piece of cake. At first, the girls remained silent. Then Alyssa tapped her manicured fingertips on the table and said, "Kit knows about your little crush on him, Mina." She dropped her ditz-façade. "But sadly, you'll always be his best friend."

The fork fell out of Mina's hand. She summoned every brain cell in her head to quickly think of a witty comeback.

"I know that. A guy can have many girlfriends, but he'll only have one best friend."

Alyssa arched a brow and ran her finger over her glossy bottom lip. "You think you're so smart and witty don't you? Well, guess what. Kit is in love with his girlfriend. Not his best friend."

Ouch. Before Mina could think of a retort, Kit returned to the table.

"What are you girls talking about?"

Alyssa twirled her hair. "*Meena* was just telling me how happy she is for her best friend. She and I will get along just fine, right Meena?" To Kit, Alyssa smiled. To Mina, she smirked.

"Right." Mina shrugged. Knowing Kit wasn't oblivious to her feelings surprised her. Using Alyssa to reject her, Kit disappointed Mina. She would have been less disappointed if Alyssa really were a harmless bimbo. Mina stared at Kit, wondering why the boy of her dreams couldn't see through Alyssa's delicious exterior into her rotten core.

And why he chose to hurt me like this on my birthday.

TWO

Half an hour later, Mina left Bubble Café, trailing behind Kit and Alyssa. Alyssa locked her arm around Kit's and pulled him toward the street curb.

"Take me shopping, Kitty-Kit. I need a new dress for a charity ball next weekend." Alyssa waved her hand to catch a cabbie's attention.

"But I had promised Mina I would spend the day with her," Kit said. Alyssa pulled his arm and pouted.

Kit gave Alyssa a signal with his eyes before he faced Mina. "Want to go shopping too, Min?"

Mina shook her head, her face expressionless. "You know I don't like to go shopping. Besides, I have to run some errands for Mom. You guys go ahead and have fun." She smiled, the corners of her eyes unwrinkled.

Kit's eyes brightened. "Are you sure about that, Min?"

Mina tipped her head, avoiding eye contact.

"Okay. I'll see you later then." Kit smiled, holding Alyssa's hand.

Mina waved and turned away. Her legs brought her halfway down the block in seconds. Tomorrow, her eyes would be puffy from crying. For now, she forced her tear ducts to behave. She'd rather wrestle a hobo than cry in front of Alyssa and Kit.

Why can't you run after me and tell me you've made a mistake, Kit? That you're not superficial like all the other boys- it's the inside that is what matters to you, not how girls look. Isn't it?

Mina turned around and saw Kit and Alyssa enter a cab they had just flagged. Kit didn't even look Mina's way.

I guess if you're happy, then I'm happy, Kit. She couldn't even convince her to believe herself.

The minute the cab disappeared, tears rolled down Mina's cheeks.

She ran down into a subway station to take the orange-line train home. Numb from heartbreak, Mina sat next to a bum wrapped in fifteen layers, who smelled of rancid clothes and garbage bags for the entire ride. In vain, the bum tried to chit-chat with Mina. No one had ever sat next to him on the train before-most people wouldn't even ride in the same compartment with him. Seeing Mina cry, he offered her his own black hankie. It was whiter than Alyssa's teeth when he had found it.

"You know how us folks like to tell people *the end is near?* Well, let me tell you one thing, sonny-boy," said the bum with a high-pitched voice. "This is just the beginning." He smiled at her and she saw his gross teeth. Oddly, this weird conversation gave her hope.

Mina pumped her fists, blowing her nose into the bum's handkerchief. "You're right. I'm not giving up on Kit that easily."

~*~

Half a block away from home, Mina couldn't believe what her dried eyes saw. She cussed, spotting blood splashed all over the porch and front door of her house.

"What the heck?"

She dashed toward her mother who stood by the door. Kaila Lin held a wet, reddened sponge in one hand and a metal bucket of water in the other.

"Are you hurt, Mom?" Mina ran her hands over her thin mother's body, searching for any gushing wounds. "Where did this blood come from? Did you call the police?"

Kaila placed the bucket and sponge on the floor. "This isn't blood. It's red paint. Don't ask me any more questions. Your squeaky voice is giving me a headache." Kaila wrinkled her nose and sniffed her daughter. "And you smell like a dumpster."

Mina sniffed herself, trying to see if Kaila's nose functioned correctly. "What are you talking about? I smell like peaches."

"Rotten ones, yes," Kaila agreed. Just help me clean before the neighbors see this mess." With that, Kaila entered the house.

Mina scrubbed the paint off the door and porch for the next hour and a half. When her hands and shoulder joints grew sore, she stopped scrubbing, even though ugly spots of red residue remained.

Mina entered her house and confronted her mother in the living room. Kaila had taken a nap while Mina cleaned up her mess. Drool made her chin shine.

"Now can we talk?" Mina asked, prodding Kaila's bony shoulder.

Kaila opened her eyes and stretched her arms and neck. She wiped her chin and smacked her lips together.

"I'm hungry. Did you cook dinner yet?" She yawned and massaged the dark, puffy circles beneath her eyes. Whenever she looked like a zombie, it meant she hadn't slept a wink the night before. Mina could also safely assume that also meant she had spent the entire night and early morning playing mahjong marathons. Illegal parlors disguised as legit-stores in Chinatown of East Uptown hosted mahjong marathons. Kaila Lin

During these marathon games, Kaila would lose an average of at least a hundred bucks a night—on bad nights.

"You've already forgotten about the paint?" Mina waved her reddened palms in front of her mother's face. "Tell me what happened or you're starving tonight."

Kaila pouted like a lazy child forced to finish her homework before she could have candy or play videogames. "Oh, alright. The agency sent some *tough* boys over. Like splashing some red paint on our porch is going to scare me. Ha!"

"Agency? You mean loan sharks? Don't tell me the boys were debt collectors." Mina pressed her throbbing temples, dreading a migraine even the strongest aspirin wouldn't fix.

"Bingo! They were, but don't worry dear. I'm not worried at all, so you shouldn't be either. Besides, I didn't borrow that much money this time." *As if that made it alright.* Kaila yawned again and looked as if nothing could faze her, not even if the leaky ceiling crashed down on her.

"How much did you borrow, then?" Mina tapped her foot, wondering which layer of *diyu*, hell, she would end down in if she strangled her mother.

Five years ago, they had swapped their mother-daughter roles.

Kaila, unable to accept the sudden death of her husband, developed a gambling addiction to escape reality. She had resigned from her job, forgetting she had to take care of her eleven-year-old daughter who was also in mourning for a lost father.

The only reason why they weren't living on the streets was because the government had supported them after Kaila gambled away her husband's life insurance payout money.

Mina had forced herself to grow up overnight. For the past five years, she had juggled schoolwork, part-time jobs, and running the household. She cooked, cleaned, made repairs, changed the light bulbs, paid the bills, and weeded the yard. Sometimes, Mina wondered if she worked harder than most of the mothers in the neighborhood as Kaila's unpaid maid.

"What are you cooking tonight? If you don't want to cook, we can order a spicy sausage pizza." Kaila licked her lips and reached for the phone.

"We'll eat the leftovers in the fridge." Mina grabbed the phone out of her mother's hand. "Stop trying to change the topic. How much money do you owe them this time?"

Kaila looked away. She brushed back long silky black bangs from her face. Mina looked nothing like her lithe, pretty mother. Instead, Mina looked more like her father, Brian Lin, who had a wild mop of hair, a rounded face (not heart-shaped), almond-shaped eyes, and freckles.

Kaila opened her hand, fanning her fingers so that Mina could see the amount. Mina wished each finger didn't mean a hundred bucks.

"Five what? Five hundred dollars?" Mina glared at her mother. *There went most of her earnings.* That was what Kaila had owed the loan sharks two months ago at the mahjong parlor.

Kaila shook her head.

Mina clasped her hand over her sticky forehead. "Five thousand dollars?" *I am going to commit mother-cide.*

Kaila shook her head again.

Mina sucked in a deep breath of air. She had a feeling she would soon suffer a complete mental and physical breakdown.

"Fifty-thousand dollars, Mina. That's how much I owe the stupid agency." Kaila patted her rumbling belly. She checked her nails and clicked her teeth.

Mina's knees buckled. "You're kidding, right? How did you lose that much playing mahjong?"

"I didn't. Last month, I tried my luck at Bowing Monkey. At first, I kept winning. I won a thousand dollars on one game of pai gow. A thousand bucks!" Kaila's eyes widened, clapping her hands together. "Then I lost everything. So I borrowed some money from an in-house agency, thinking I could win enough in one night to secure your future. All that time, I was thinking about you, you know."

Right.

Bowing Monkey, Unseen Phoenix was an unsanctioned, underground casino in the bowels of Chinatown. If Mina knew the location of the casino, she would alert the cops. If she could burn the place down with no repercussion, she would.

"No, I didn't know you were that selfless." Mina could mope, sigh, scream and act like a drama queen, but that wouldn't solve anything.

"Do you have a copy of the loan contract? What's the loan term? The interest rate? How much do you owe them this month?" Mina readied her mental calculator. The last time Kaila had owed money, Mina made the entire payment the next day, spending every penny of her personal savings.

This time around, I'll probably have to sell a few organs to pay off Mom's debt. I could sell all my ovaries. Five-grand a pop!

"Don't worry about any of that. I'll be able to pay them back by the end of the month." Kaila stood up and stretched out her body like a feline. She removed a pack of smokes from her shorts pocket and lit up a cigarette.

"With what money?" Mina snatched the cancer-stick out of her mother's hand and crushed it in the ashtray on the cracked glass surface of the coffee table. Kaila lit up another cigarette and puffed it like a rebel.

"With the money I'll get from selling this dump, of course." Kaila blew a sorry-excuse for a ring of smoke at her daughter's face. Mina coughed and her eyes watered. She karate-chopped the second cigarette out of Kaila's mouth, determined to be able to breathe in her own home.

"You're not selling the house, Mom." Silence enveloped them.

Their house could pass for a haunted house-the roof leaked, the floorboards creaked, and the walls and ceiling had mice in them. The rusty pipes needed changing and the gas stoves could combust at anytime. Their shoddy, secondhand furniture pieces were over a decade old. Asbestos and lead paint were probably in the mix. Despite all of this, Mina loved their house. It held a million happy memories of her beloved dad.

The house was a century-year old fix-up he had bought to renovate. But before he could start the renovations, he passed away.

"Why do you always do everything I hate? I won't let you sell Daddy's house."

"The house belongs to me. My name is on the deed. Yours isn't. Tomorrow, I'm meeting with a real estate agent. When I sell the house, I'll pay off all my debts." Kaila's breath reeked of smoke and alcohol when she neared her daughter. She placed a clammy hand on Mina's arm. "I'll even put aside some money for your college tuition. You think I don't love you, but I do."

You stopped loving me five years ago.

Mina brushed her mother's hand away from her arm. She raised her chin. "The moment you have more money, you'll just gamble it away. You're not selling Daddy's house. I will put myself up for adoption if you do." Mina blinked and fat teardrops rolled down the side of her face. "Give me some time. I'll find a way to pay off your debt."

"Tell me, sweetie. What can a fifteen-year old girl do in the Uptown to make fifty thousand dollars in a month? Whore herself? Strip? Maybe you could, if you were prettier." Kaila waggled her finger at her daughter. "Win the lottery? Find a Prince Charming? Inherit money from long-lost relatives who just happen to be royals?" Kaila chortled, mocking her daughter's hope. "Only in storybooks! I'm selling the house and that's final."

Sixteen years ago, Kaila Lin had a C-section, bringing Mina into the world. Today, she had forgotten it was her only child's birthday.

"Give me one month and I'll think of something. I know I will." Mina stared at her mother with unblinking, conviction-filled eyes. "Please? Did you buy me a present today, Mom?"

"Why would I buy you a present?" Kaila chewed on her finger and spat out a hangnail. "What's the occasion?" "It's my birthday. I was fifteen yesterday."

"Oh. Right."

If she had no pride, Mina would drop to her knees to beg. "Consider giving me one month as my birthday gift. Mom, please?"

Kaila patted her belly. "Fine. I'll have to talk to the agency about this. Are you happy now? Do you like your birthday present? Happy birthday, darling. Now go make us dinner. I'm starving." Kaila ushered her daughter into the kitchen. Mina wrapped a red apron around her sweaty body.

Guess this means I don't even have time to be heartbroken. How many organs will I have to sell to make fifty-grand?

THREE

The next day, at half past noon, after searching all over South Uptown for a well-paying summer job in vain, Mina ended up loitering on Cherry Street in front of Trendy Star. The useless fifty-buck gift card Kit and the fake-bimbo had given her took up too much pocket space.

Mina wondered if she could exchange the card for money. Fifty dollars was, after all, point-one percent of fifty-grand.

This morning, she had hoped everything that had happened yesterday was a nightmare. When she picked up the loan contract Kaila had signed, Mina knew her reality was worse than any nightmare.

Entering Trendy Star, she felt like a penguin in a chicken coop. Tall and model-thin fashionistas rifled through the clothing racks. None of the well-dressed shop attendants greeted Mina. She walked to the back counter and dropped the gift card on the glass surface.

"Hi. Can I exchange this for money?" Mina flashed her anti-Chiclets teeth.

The brunette behind the counter arched her freshly plucked eyebrow. "Are you kidding me, Miss? Everyone knows you can't exchange a gift card for money." She picked up the card and handed it back to Mina. "By the way, we carry plus-sizes upstairs."

Zing. Ouch. Mina shook her head. "No thanks. Besides, I'm just a size ten."

"Just a size ten. Wow, congrats. Next please." The size negative-one brunette rolled her eyes and greeted the pretty customer behind Mina with a bright smile.

Mina decided to wait in line for a nice customer to buy the gift card from her. Half an hour later, she could have turned into a naked marble statue and no one would have noticed. Even though everyone on the line had bought more than fifty bucks worth of clothing, no one offered to help her. With an invisible tail between her legs, she walked out of the boutique.

Crossing the street, Mina didn't hear loud honking from a speeding car. She only noticed it when the car panic-braked, stopping a centimeter away from sending her flying down the street.

Hyperventilating, Mina clutched her chest and just stared at the driver behind the wheel.

~*~

Jaiden Daniels's face blanched. The son of Jameson Daniels, Comptroller of the Uptown and billionaire CEO of Daniels Limited Partnership (D.L.P.), almost killed a girl with his new, one of a kind modified, crimson Maserati. Jaiden stared back at her- she looked like a dazed bumpkin about to be beamed into a UFO.

Mina's heart stopped for a second.

She analyzed the shiny sports car. She had a feeling the young driver could sell the car and buy a two-bedroom co-op in West Uptown with the money.

How could someone so young be so rich?

The driver wore stylish shades over his eyes and had slicked back black hair. Mina almost wished his car had hit her. Instead of selling her organs, she could make a heap of money from a lawsuit settlement.

The driver behind Jaiden honked. Reflexively, Jaiden honked as well.

Mina jumped.

How obnoxious! He almost killed me and now he wants me to get off the streets?

The cogwheels in her head turned. She listened to the evil advice of the little Mina-Devil on her left shoulder.

Pretend you're hurt. Sue his pants off. Save Daddy's house.

17

Alright. I'll probably regret this later, but here goes. How else am I going to make fifty-grand?

Jaiden cussed when the girl dropped to the ground, blocking his escape route. He visualized his near future.

Soon, the girl would create a citywide traffic jam. The police would arrive, along with the paparazzi. In less than an hour's time, Jaiden would ruin his father's name, reputation, and chance of becoming the Mayor.

Tomorrow's headline would be similar to the following: **Comptroller's Son Almost Killed a Girl. Possible Drug Use Involved.**

Which wouldn't be true, since Jaiden Daniels never touches drugs.

In return, Jameson Daniels would confiscate every one of Jaiden's cars and motorcycles. He would also have an excuse to send Jaiden to Charlesburg Academy, a prestigious institution in Edinburgh. In the Academy, scholarly prigs would brainwash Jaiden into a conforming and respectable young man.

Kind of like a male version of a Stepford wife, Jaiden mused.

He got out of his car and walked toward the girl. She lay down supine; her eyelids squeezed shut and twitching. From the way her chest rose, he could tell she had no trouble breathing. He prodded the girl's sides with the tip of his dark brown alligator skin loafer. She winced.

Jaiden chuckled. Like any other typical Uptowner, she was ready to sue anything and anyone for big bucks.

Just like how those people tried to sue Mickey D's for making them fat.

Jaiden knelt down beside the girl and scooped her up in his arms. She weighed even heavier than she looked. Carrying her, he thought his spine would snap in two.

What the hell? Why is he carrying me? Why isn't he calling 911? Mina caught a whiff of his cologne-he smelled soapy clean, with a hint of distinctly masculine spice. He reminded her of an ocean. Kit had a distinguishing smell too—woodland scent.

Oh Kit…

Addicted to his scent, whenever she had a chance, Mina tried to sniff Kit's clothes. Mina's nose itched-she held back a sneeze to avoid blowing her own cover.

Jaiden eased Mina onto the sidewalk. He squeezed his fingers over her wrist.

"Pulse is normal." He placed a finger over her nostrils.

"Breathing regularly. There are no visible cuts, blood, or bruising." Jaiden smirked, using the lingo and actions of suave TV doctors.

"There's only one test left." He squeezed her nose and clasped his hand over her mouth.

Crap! He knows! He's suffocating me! Mina could pretend to pass out. But before she could do so, she would have really passed out. She could feel herself turning blue. Unable to keep up her act, she gasped for air and pried the guy's hand away from her mouth and nose.

Jaiden laughed. "I guess this means you're okay. Ciao."

Mina coughed and sat up. Pointing at him, she said, "You nearly killed me."

"What are you, a drama queen? I do suggest you take some acting classes first." Jaiden stood up and removed his shades. He stared at Mina with violet-blue eyes, framed by dark soot lashes. With an aristocrat's sharp nose, defined cheekbones, and eyes that could belong to hot vampires (not the ones that sparkle in the sun like diamonds though, ack), the guy before her looked like a celebrity.

Or Prince Charming.

As handsome as he was, Mina had a feeling he was probably completely maggot-infested on the inside like Alyssa.

"Plus, the keyword here is *nearly*." Jaiden arched his eyebrow. Like other girls, he knew this one here couldn't resist his charms. Jaiden ran his fingers through his hair and cleared his throat. He glanced at his red-faced Parmigiani Fleurier watch. "I don't have time to deal with a malingerer. I assume it's money you want, right?" Jaiden took out his dark red leather wallet and removed five crisp hundred-dollar bills. He dropped the money on the ground next to Mina. Mina hesitated before taking the money.

She wanted to smack the little Mina-Devil on her shoulder.

Since when did I become such a horrible person? What am I, a con artist?

Before Mina could apologize to the guy and give him back his money, he disappeared into his car and drove away. She rubbed the money together in her hands and waited for her palms to burn.

Oh well. At least now I have one percent of the money Mom owes. Mom should be convinced I could pay off her debts if I give her this money.

She stood up, patting her dusty behind. Turning to walk away, she noticed a silver mirror on the ground. She hesitated, but picked it up anyway. It was only then she realized it was a smartphone and not a mirror.

Rich Boy must have dropped it. I guess the least I can do is return it to him.

Mina played around with the nifty piece of technology in her hand, hoping she could find some clues as to where the guy lived and who he was. The screen lit up and a shocking picture popped on screen.

Mina dropped the phone. "My god."

FOUR

Fifteen minutes later, Jaiden walked into D.L.P.'s main corporate building in the center of South Uptown.

He reached into his trouser pocket for his smartphone, only to realize he had lost it.

Great. That silly girl must have it.

In the elevator riding to the thirtieth floor, Jaiden adjusted his white shirt collar and cuffs. He removed his shades and smoothed back his gelled hair. With long strides and a straightened back, he entered the CEO's office.

Jameson Daniels's city office was less spectacular. This was why he spent most of his time in this office, where he ran his own company and watched over the city's finances. Behind his desk, the large ceiling-high windows offered a spectacular view of the city.

Jaiden groaned and felt his spine tingle the minute he stepped into the office. At the obsidian desk, sat his father and Michael Helwick, CEO of Helwick Incorporated.

Michael was a longtime business partner and friend of Jaiden's father. Not only was he a business guru and a finance-genius, he was the city's Mayor and the candidate most slated to win the seat again this November.

His opponent had had his eye on the mayoral seat for years. Jameson ran against his friend.

In the Uptown, few men stood on a pedestal higher than Jameson. Michael was one of them.

The middle-aged men greeted Jaiden with controlled smiles. Jameson waved for his son to take a seat next to Michael. Unlike Jameson, Michael was short and stout, like a teapot, balding and pale. Jameson looked like a weathered version of Jaiden, with dark blue eyes and streaks of white and gray in his thick black hair.

"We were just talking about you, son." Jameson sat back. "Michael tells me Madison will be spending the summer here in the city."

Jameson's mentioning of Madison's name made his son shudder.

"She misses you so much, my dear boy." Michael wiped his sweaty double chin with a handkerchief. "She constantly talks about how you two used to play together. How time flies."

The older men chatted about the good old days. Jaiden feigned interest, trying not to look bored.

"I can't believe it, but they're old enough to get married now." Michael chuckled.

"Michael means you two are old enough to technically get married, to whomever you two please," Jameson added. The two older men shot each other knowing glances.

Just like women. Jaiden rolled his eyes, and daydreamed of being able to snap his fingers and disappear like Houdini. For years, Michael and Jameson (more Michael than Jameson) had hinted they wanted to become future in-laws. For years, Jaiden had dreaded this.

"So, I would highly appreciate it if you can keep her company this summer-she's been away for so long, the city is almost foreign to her," Michael said.

Jaiden glared at his father, giving him a you-owe-me-big-time look.

How is it possible that the Uptown's Mayor's daughter feels like a foreigner?

Jaiden bowed his head at Michael. "It would be my pleasure."

"Excellent." Michael tapped his fingers together, like a corpulent version of Mr. Burns. "Madison will be downstairs shortly. You probably won't recognize her anymore."

I doubt that, Jaiden muttered in his head. A few years ago, Madison Helwick was a female version of her father, with a mop of oily auburn hair and a crater-filled face that could make the moon's surface green with envy. As children, Jaiden teased her. Despite his bullying, Madison had always been his number-one fan.

"Excuse me." Michael whipped out his ringing smartphone and answered it. When the call ended, he grinned at Jaiden and patted his shoulder.

"My Madi is in the lobby waiting. Have fun."

"Oh, I will." Jaiden turned and pressed his lips together at his father. Jameson

shrugged.

The older gentlemen resumed their fond reflection of the good old days. Jaiden stepped out of his father's office sighing.

Shouldn't mayoral candidates be unfriendly and bitter toward each other? Why are those two so chummy? Even their campaigns against each other were benign instead of smear.

Jaiden imagined an eighteen-year-old Madison to be a three hundred pound walrus with the fashion sense of a clown.

To his surprise, his eyes enjoyed the sight of a young woman standing in the D.L.P. lobby. Tall, lithe, and stunning were words that described Madison. Her auburn hair was short in an A-line bob style. In a classy white dress-suit and three-inch heels, Madison looked like she had just stepped out of a Vogue magazine. She tilted her head and smiled.

"Hello, love," she said with a French, nasally accent. Three years in a Paris boarding school did wonders for her, he thought.

"I missed you." Her scent invaded Jaiden's nostrils-fragrant jasmine and roses.

"Madi?" Jaiden rubbed the back of his neck. "You look good." Though he didn't lie, he did have wonder how much Michael had spent to make her look this amazing. He could easily see that her sharp, straight nose wasn't the one God had given her.

Madison batted her green eyes and licked her plush bottom lip. Collagen injections, Jaiden guessed.

"Thanks. I like what I see too. You're as handsome as ever. Like Adonis." She sauntered over to him and gave him a kiss on the cheek before wrapping an arm around his. "We have a lot of catching up to do. First, you have to take me somewhere fun, Jai-Jai."

"Somewhere fun? Want to play Space-Tennis? It's tennis played in a zero gravity court. They just opened up a place in West Uptown."

Madison shook her head. The mini-chandelier diamond earrings hanging from her earlobes jangled.

"No? How about horseback riding? Skydiving?"

Madison waggled her finger. "We're adults now, Jaiden. Let's do something fun adults do."

"Oh? What did you have in mind?" Jaiden tilted his head, ready for any game the plastic socialite wanted to play.

~*~

That night, Mina dangled her feet off the rooftop of her house and counted five stars in the sky. Last summer, she had spent every night atop the roof stargazing with Kit. Whenever Kit fell asleep, Mina would stare at him and her fingers would itch to caress his flawless face.

It's not fair that he's so beautiful.

She looked at the house next door, unable to find her best friend at home. *He's probably out with Alyssa again.* Mina wondered if the butterflies in Alyssa's stomach did somersaults whenever she was near Kit. And if she knew at this moment she was the luckiest girl in the world.

Ripping her mind away from thoughts of Kit, Mina wondered what she should do to save her house.

She couldn't exactly smile.

She took out Rich Boy's smartphone and looked at the nasty picture again.

Should I call the cops? Or…

On the bright screen flashed a mutilated bald doll head with bloody eyes. The doll's blood-smeared lips smiled, making it look like a masochist. The red-font message under the image was:

Death to the Daniels. The boy goes first.

If this isn't a death-threat, then I can strut down any haute-couture catwalk and pose as a supermodel.

In the Uptown, only one famous family was associated with the name Daniels- Jameson Daniels and his son, the boy in the message, Jaiden Daniels, a.k.a. snooty Rich Boy in the red sports car that almost killed Mina.

Asides from being an active political figure, Jameson Daniels owned a corporation, D.L.P., which had invested in multiple businesses in the Uptown.

After scourging the web for information, Mina discovered Jameson Daniels's net worth was eight point eight billion dollars, slated to rise to nine billion before the end of the year.

How many zeroes are in a billion? Sheesh. He wouldn't think twice about spending fifty-grand to ensure his son's safety, right?

Jameson Daniels dealt with the Uptown's budget, finances, and audited city agencies and businesses. He also managed eight hundred city employees-surely not all of them were happy with their affluent and powerful boss.

Naturally, Jameson Daniels had made enemies. Even the Mayor could be a suspect since Jameson was a mayoral candidate.

A brilliant idea launched in Mina's head. Instead of alerting the cops, she decided to handle this threat for the Daniels.

I don't have what it takes to be Sherlock. But I can be a great bodyguard. Rich Boy could use someone like me by his side to handle blackmailers and kidnappers, the likes.

Mina climbed down the roof and practiced Mina-Jitsu on her front lawn, a form of martial arts she had created. Mina-Jitsu was just one of Mina's obsessions. She grew up watching Jackie Chan, Jet Li, and Bruce Lee films with her father. Mina-Jitsu consisted of moves she had stolen/borrowed from the masters in the movies.

After an hour of sparring with the air, Mina belly-flopped down on the grass and closed her eyes, dreaming about the perfect plan she would soon have.

I hope my plan works. I'd rather have a sex change than lose Daddy's house to loan sharks.

The next morning, she rode her bike to North Uptown, a gated community in the city where only the wealthy lived.

According to the web sources, Jameson Daniels lived on Eighteen Richmond Lane.

With the plethora of information on the Internet, anyone who could browse the web could become a private detective.

Or to become a super-stalker.

Mina also discovered how she could easily infiltrate North Uptown without a special pass or an invitation from the inhabitants. All she had to do was pose as a delivery girl. She tied her unruly hair in a thick ponytail. Dressed in a black vest, white shirt, black pants and old black shoes two sizes too small for her chubby feet, Mina looked just like a waitress from a Chinese restaurant. Instead of takeout food, she had Jaiden's smartphone in a brown paper bag.

She stopped her bike by the guard booth at the gates.

"Welcome to North Uptown. State your business please," said a bored-looking guard inside the booth. He yawned and poked his head out to study Mina.

"I'm from the Phoenix Garden Restaurant. I'm here to deliver food to Eighteen Richmond Lane," she stuttered. Mina hoped her nose didn't twitch too much and the guard couldn't read body language well. She forced herself to look him straight in the eye. A trick she had learned was to stare at the area between a person's eyes when she didn't feel comfortable enough to make direct eye contact.

The guard tilted his head. "The Daniels ordered takeout? Strange." The guard narrowed his eyes. Mina gulped, trying not to appear nervous.

It would have really helped if there had been information on the websites she had found about how the Daniels didn't like takeout.

"Fine. Go right ahead and take a left on the next street."

"Thanks." Mina smiled at the inept guard and biked in through the opened gates toward Richmond Lane. Every home she passed was an impressive looking storybook mansion, but none was as magnificent as Eighteen Richmond Lane.

Open-mouthed, Mina parked her bike in front of a large pool-fountain in the middle of an expansive stretch of green lawn. The grass beneath her feet was so green and perfectly cut that it seemed unnatural.

Dogs would kill to do their business here.

She wiped her sweaty face and eyes. The two-story mansion and side structures combined measured at least fifty thousand square feet. Each bedroom was probably the size of her entire house.

Judging from the number of modern-styled windows, Mina estimated the second floor had at least fifteen bedrooms and maybe more.

The manse was an architect's dream, especially its Corinthian-styled pillars.

Four cars, one silver-white limo, and three motorcycles occupied the open driveway. Seeing the red sports car from yesterday, Mina knew this was exactly where Rich Boy lived.

She walked toward the twelve-foot tall white front door and

rang the doorbell. Twenty seconds later, the door opened and a bald man in a black suit greeted Mina. Mina arched her neck. He had to be at least six feet three inches tall.

He bowed his head. "How may I help you?" His tone was low and raspy. His face, devoid of emotion and wrinkles, made him look robotic.

The rich could afford robot-servants, after all.

He pressed his lips together, studying Mina's outfit. "Are you the temp-maid from the agency, Miss?"

"Uh…" Before Mina could tell the bald man no, he pulled her into the manse, taking her silence as an answer to "yes."

"You're a little early, but that's a good sign. You also look young. Then again, looks can be deceiving. My name is Bunion and I am the Butler. You are?"

"Mina Lin." Mina shook the man's massive hand. Just like that, Bunion hired her, it appeared.

"A pleasure to make your acquaintance, Miss Lin. Please follow me."

Mina welcomed the sight of the sheer grandeur of the mansion. A long carpeted hall stood before her. To the left of the hall was a white spiraling staircase with shiny golden handrails. A diamond chandelier hung from the ceiling. Famous looking paintings lined the walls.

Isn't that an authentic Monet? If she didn't know these people had money before, she knew now.

Walking along the hallway, Bunion showed Mina the main living room, complete with a fireplace and black leather furniture and a hundred-inch LED screen.

"This is the Red Room. Every room in the manse has a name, by the way."

"Nice." She hoped her one-word answer wouldn't come off as rude. She could only stare at the room dazed, as if she had stepped into a fairytale castle. Mina almost forgot why she was here and that she wasn't the temp-maid the Daniels had hired.

The next stop was the Black Pool Room, an entertainment and bar room with a nine foot long red pool table in the center. A corner bar with black marble counters held an impressive collection of decades-old wines and liquors.

Next to the Black Pool Room was a gym room filled with treadmills, bikes, elliptical machines and weights that could make a stick-thin man turn into a buff beefcake.

Afterward, Bunion led Mina into a storage room filled with linens and tools. "This is where the clean linens, brooms, mops, and vacuums are. Take whatever you need here."

Mina looked inside the closet. The amount of linens inside closet could fill an entire section at Macy's.

Further down the hallway, Bunion took Mina to a room hidden behind a door disguised as a nine-foot tall painting of snow-capped mountains.

Bunion waved Mina inside the room. "Finally, this room is called the White Piano Room. This is our Young Master's favorite room."

Rich Boy's favorite room? Mina inspected every corner of the White Piano Room. In the center of the room rested a white grand piano. To the far left was a long lounging cream sofa next to a crystal-surfaced coffee table. Atop the table was a beautiful porcelain vase filled with fragrant white orchids with purplish-red centers.

"Since you'll be the Young Master's maid, there are some rules you shall follow. First, make sure this room is spotless everyday. The Young Master will not play the piano if the keys are oily."

"Got it." *That's right, Min. Just play along. Being a Daniels's maid will make everything else easier. Being Rich Boy's maid? Even better!*

"Next. The Young Master wakes up every morning at exactly nine. By nine-thirty, his breakfast must be in his bedroom. Sometimes, the Young Master eats in the dining room or the gardens. Let me show you the kitchen and then we'll go to the second floor."

Bunion led Mina into the kitchen at the end of the hallway.

Mina wondered if the Daniels had imported a kitchen from a five-star hotel. The large walk-in stainless steel refrigerator in the center of the kitchen could house a small family, Mina decided. It was bigger than an igloo,

Busy chefs hustled around the kitchen as if they were late in preparing a feast for a royal family. Bunion whistled as he popped a ripe strawberry into his mouth. He introduced Mina to the other employees. Then he handed Mina a heavy platter.

"Every morning, you are to make sure the platter is complete with coffee, grapefruit juice, bird's nest congee, brown sugar on sliced avocado and honey on toast. Check, check, and check. Got it?"

Mina thought all the food on the platter seemed too delicate for a young man. Maybe she should taste-test the food for him first. She licked her lips. "I got it."

"The agency had said you were the best of the best. The Young Master may be picky, but I'm sure you'll do a fine job. I can tell because you even brought your own uniform." Bunion winked.

Mina grinned. Lady Luck finally liked her. "Just how picky is Jaiden?"

Bunion waggled his finger. "You must address him as your *Young Master*."

You're kidding, right, Mina wanted to say.

"Let's just say you're the tenth maid hired for him this year." Bunion sighed before he became expressionless. "Do you have any other questions?"

Nose twitching, Mina beamed. "Since I'm a professional maid, I have no questions." She covered the platter with a lid before balancing it on her arms, marching out of the kitchen behind Bunion.

I'm a pro-maid; thanks to all the pro-bono maid training I get at home.

"Let's go upstairs then," Bunion said.

At the top of the spiraling stairway, Mina stepped onto a long hallway, her feet sinking into plush royal blue carpeting. Water flowed down the stone walls—waterfall walls. Mina arched her neck up and looked at the ceiling, a holographic projection displaying the real-time sky.

"The last room to the left is the Young Master's room. At this time, he should be expecting his breakfast."

Mina bowed her head and smiled. "Alright. Thanks, Bunion."

"You're welcome. See you later, and good luck."

Bunion made his way down the stairs, leaving Mina alone in front of Jaiden's bedroom. She inhaled three deep breaths and braced herself to confront the guy who had almost killed her yesterday.

Will he recognize me? She knocked on the door and pushed it open, not waiting for an answer from him.

Fifteen minutes ago, Jaiden stretched his arms overhead and rolled out of bed. Having spent the entire day with Madison yesterday, he overslept this morning.

And all they had done was shop, talk, and eat.

Never in his life had he carried ten filled shopping bags in each arm and walked through the Uptown like the socialite's personal assistant.

If asked, he would admit he had expected to do something else fun adults did with Madi. He wasn't exactly disappointed, but he would never have guessed that in Madison's book, adults went shopping for fun. After shopping, they had lunch, dinner, and midnight dessert. She didn't leave him alone until one in the morning.

He took a quick shower in the bathroom adjacent to his bedroom. He combed his hair, shaved his face and brushed his teeth. Fifteen minutes later, he entered his bedroom, wearing nothing but a dark blue towel wrapped around his torso and thighs.

Jaiden had forgotten that a temp-maid would come in today, since he had been maid-less for the past week. About to remove the towel to change into fresh clothes, he heard a gasp. At his doorway stood a wavy-haired, openmouthed female pervert. She dropped his breakfast platter and bolted away.

Jaiden grumbled, clumsily putting on his clothes. Three minutes later, red as a beet, he stormed outside to confront his highly unprofessional new maid.

FIVE

Mina stood at the end of the hallway with her legs shoulder-width apart. She positioned her hands to fight. She had no idea why she felt so embarrassed. So what if Rich Boy had six-pack abs and muscular legs? So what if she had almost seen him completely nudey-pants? And so what if she stared at his body agape for a little too long?

Calm down, Mina!

Jaiden squinted. Glaring at Mina, recognition sparked in his eyes.

"Are you stalking me? Five hundred dollars wasn't enough? You know I can easily have you arrested for trespassing on private property."

Mina relaxed herself and reached into her pant pocket for the bag with Jaiden's smartphone. She took the phone out and waved it. "I came to give this back to you."

Jaiden grabbed his smartphone out of her hand.

"Look at your newest picture message," Mina said.

Jaiden glanced at the image on the screen of his phone. He made a face. "Don't tell me, this is another one of your scams to make fast money. Very childish. Red paint on a doll's head?"

"I'm sorry, but I'm not a sicko. I will admit I desperately need money though. Listen, I can help you. This is a serious threat. It says death to the Daniels."

"I know. I can read." Jaiden tilted his head.

"Look, I can protect you from the person who's sending the threat." Mina hoped the way she flexed her biceps could convince Rich Boy.

Jaiden snorted. "Even if my life really is in danger, why would I need you to protect me? I have bodyguards and the security in the manse is flawless."

"If you're so well-protected, then how come I'm standing right here right now?" Mina jutted out her chin.

Jaiden scratched his chin. "A fluke. Bunion let you in?"

"Your butler thought I was the new maid and he let me in, no questions asked."

"Then Bunion will be reprimanded. Thanks for bringing this back to me, but if you're expecting a reward, then I'll have to disappoint you." Jaiden waggled his finger, taunting Mina as if she were a child.

Without a warning, Mina ran toward Jaiden and caught him in a headlock jujitsu-masters would be proud of. Like a pro-wrestler, she brought Jaiden down into a kneeling position. She twisted his arms behind his back.

"Hey!" Jaiden almost whimpered, trying to fight back against her arms.

"Where are your bodyguards now, Rich Boy? Who's going to save you?" Mina tightened her hold.

Jaiden could not believe a girl who looked like a fluffy marshmallow could take him down with such little effort. He struggled to break free.

Almost breathless, he said, "Alright, alright-let go of me, She-Hulk."

"So you'll hire me as your bodyguard?" Eyes brightened, Mina released Jaiden. He shot up to stand and looked at Mina as if she had an orange-sized wart between her eyes.

Jaiden massaged his aching shoulders. "Tell me why you need money so badly first and maybe I'll consider."

Mina bit her bottom lip, wondering if she should just tell him the truth. "I have to help pay off my mother's gambling debts. Otherwise, she'll sell our house and-"

"You'll live on the streets." Sob stories-Jaiden had heard them all. In the past decade, his father had donated over a hundred million dollars to various charities.

"You look like you don't believe me." Mina crossed her arms.

The last thing Jaiden wanted to do was anger the She-Hulk again. Looking at her fists, he had no doubt she could snap off his neck with one karate chop.

"No, I believe you. How much debt is your mother in?"

Mina held up five fingers. "Fifty-grand."

"That's pocket change." Jaiden stroked his chin, studying the strange sassy female specimen before him again.

Why not buy a fifty-thousand dollar new toy? To Jaiden, Mina looked like the perfect human shield and a fun new maid to torture. If someone really wanted to kill him, she could protect him.

"Alright, here's the deal. I'll hire you as my maid and bodyguard. However, you will only get one salary. It's not much, but no one has complained yet."

"I just want to be your bodyguard," Mina said, hands on her hips in full teacup mode.

"Beggars can't be choosers, Miss. Either you double as my maid or I'll have you escorted off these premises." Jaiden tapped his foot.

He's right, Mina. Beggars can't be choosers! "Okay, but how much are you paying me?"

Mimicking Mina, Jaiden held up five fingers. "Five grand, paid weekly."

"Really?" That's more than what most college graduates make in a month! Mina could run into his arms and kiss him if she weren't so shy. Before summer vacation would end, she would make enough to pay off her mother's debts. Then she reminded herself she needed fifty-grand in a month's time. Trying her luck, she asked, "Do you think I can ask for ten-weeks of salary in advance?"

Jaiden stretched his neck. "You want all fifty-grand in advance?" How typical of a con artist, scammer, and gold-digger wannabe.

"Yes, if that's possible. My mom signed a loan contract agreeing to make a full payment in a month. Guess what the loan rate is? Twenty-two percent." Mina dropped her shoulders.

Jaiden almost believed her. Lying through her teeth, she didn't look away, twitch, or appear antsy. When the girl didn't move around or pretend to be dead, she wasn't that hard on the eyes as he had first thought she was, with her wild mop of hair in a thick ponytail, impish freckles across her face, and expressive almond-shaped brown eyes. Not one part on her body was man-made.

He imagined that she would actually look presentable if she styled her hair and wore better fitting clothes.

Mina inched away from Jaiden. Boys usually didn't stare at her like this. She placed her arms over her barely-there chest. "What are you looking at?" she questioned.

"Nothing." Jaiden tilted his head. "Just wondering how someone with such flabby arms could be so strong."

Mina hid her arms behind her back. "They're not flabby, they're muscular. I once arm wrestled the entire football team at school and won."

That one time, Mina had wanted to impress Kit. She challenged every member of the Uptown football team to arm wrestle her after she overheard one jock state how all the girls at school were weak and dainty. If Kit weren't with her, she wouldn't have had the guts to confront of those burly jocks.

"Freakish," Jaiden muttered. Well, she would work for his bodyguard, it seemed. At least she wouldn't kill him. "Anyway, what's your name, you can start by cleaning my room. I'll have my breakfast in the gardens today. We'll talk later about your salary advance."

"Thank you so much," Mina said with genuine sincerity in her tone. Then she held out her hand, palm facing Jaiden. "But there's one thing I want to clarify. My name is Mina Lin, Jaiden. Not what's-your-name."

None of his other maids had addressed him by his first name before. Except his favorite maid—she was allowed to call him Jaiden. "Funny, you look more like a Mary Sue."

"Ha, ha, ha." Mina walked into his bedroom, eyes rolling like cheese-wheels. If she could stick Rich Boy and Alyssa in a cramped cell together, throw in an unhappy skunk, Mina would go to the local zoo to steal a skunk.

At the stairway, Jaiden bumped into Bunion who led a six-foot tall blond woman up the stairs.

Bunion panted. "My Young Master, I have made a terrible mistake. This here is your real new maid, Miss-"

"Mary," the real maid said. Her voice was deep and gruff like a manly man's.

What's her name was definitely a better choice as Jaiden's maid, even though he doubted she had any experience as a maid.

Contrary to his belief, Mina cleared up the mess she had made in his bedroom in no time before expertly making his bed and fluffing his pillows.

"Please show Miss Mary out the door, Bunion, and compensate her for her traveling expenses. I've already decided to hire the other girl." Jaiden gave Mary an apologetic look. He patted Bunion on the shoulder. "Next time you let someone in, double check her credentials first."

Bunion dropped his head in shame. "Yes, Young Master."

Jaiden grinned, disappearing downstairs. Bunion apologized to the real maid and led her out the manse. The maid shook her massive fist and cursed in a foreign language before finally stomping away.

Through the sliding glass door in the dining room, Jaiden walked to the gardens next to the waterfall pool. He sat by a round white patio table and looked at the doll head picture again, mentally making a list of suspects who could have sent the threat. Jaiden prepared himself for a long list-both he and his father had plenty of enemies in the Uptown.

Could it be the leader of the Packer's Union, who constantly protested against his father's decisions and budget cuts? Or supporters of the celebrity candidate who had lost the race for Comptroller last November?

Who could it be?

Jaiden decided he would give his phone to his private detective later.

His new maid jarred his thoughts ten minutes later when she set a second breakfast platter down on the table with a clang. She removed the silver lid and stood next to him like a cyborg.

Jaiden arched his neck. "You're done cleaning my room?"

"Yup. I just need to vacuum a bit."

Jaiden looked at his breakfast. "You know, I don't stir my own coffee. The avocado must also be sliced into perfect cubes."

Mina stirred the coffee with a silver spoon. "Do I have to use a ruler and measure the avocado cubes so they're perfect squares?"

"That would be nice and very professional of you." Jaiden beamed.

Mina cut the sliced up avocado into un-perfect cubes and jabbed a fork into a cube, handing it to Jaiden. "Do I have to feed you your breakfast too? Bring you a bib?" Wipe your butt?

"No. Just bring me the morning paper."

Mina saluted Jaiden. "Yes, boss." Having made a mental-map of the mansion earlier, Mina navigated the place with ease. She found the newspaper rolled up in the front lawn. When she picked up the paper, a knife dropped out.

She bent down and grasped the handle. The blood-covered blade glinted. Mina wrapped the paper around the knife and brought it to gardens. She removed the knife and showed it to Jaiden.

Jaiden stared at his fiendish maid brandishing a bloodied knife at him. His young life flashed before his eyes.

Mina dropped the knife on the table. "I found this in the newspaper. I told you-it's a serious threat. Are you going to call the police?"

Jaiden's voice cracked when he said, "No. I'll hire a private detective. If I notify the police, the paparazzi will be here and the whole world will know." As a political figure, the less the public knew about Jameson Daniels's problems, the better.

"Put the knife and my phone in two separate plastic bags for me and leave them in my bedroom."

"Okay." Mina hurried into the kitchen and retrieved two Ziploc bags. Back in the gardens, she placed the phone and the knife into the bags. She carried the bags back upstairs to his bedroom, working up a sweat, before planting herself beside Jaiden again.

"What else do you need, Boss?"

Jaiden grinned, admiring the way Mina worked so efficiently, though he would never admit it. He admitted that he also liked her calling him 'boss.'

"Have the White Piano Room spotless in half an hour. I have a guest to entertain shortly."

"Okie dokie." Usually, Mina would not be so subservient. Curtailing to people was not exactly her strong suit. Jaiden Daniels, however, was her ticket to saving her house. She had to show him he would not regret hiring her. As much as she hated being bossed around, she knew she had to suck up her pride and deal with whatever Rich Boy threw at her. How else would she be able to make so much money in so little time? After all, like her mother had said, she wouldn't exactly be able to become a stripper.

She tapped her forefingers together. "Before I go make the White Piano Room spotless, can we talk about my salary advance?"

Jaiden dabbed the corners of his mouth with a beige silk cloth. "You're still in your probation period. Ask me again later. I would like to finish my breakfast alone, if you don't mind."

"Not at all, Boss." Mina rushed back into the manse like a hummingbird with endless energy. Hopefully, by showing him how well she worked, her probation period would last just one day.

After gathering cleaning materials, she made the White Piano Room sparkling clean, starting with the concert-hall-worthy white piano. She wiped down each key until they reflected sunlight from the window.

She pressed a piano key down by accident. The sound it made reminded her of Kiterin.

If I knew how to play the piano, would Kit choose to be with me instead of with Alyssa?

She imagined herself playing the piano as Kit played the violin-the music they played together would be as beautiful as their love. She could see Kit now, lying atop the piano like a happy cat, admiring her play.

"I wish."

Sighing, she moved away from the piano to clean the rest of the room. She added fresh water to the flower vase, vacuumed the carpet, and even dusted the walls.

Exactly half an hour later, Jaiden walked into the room. Mina had finished cleaning everything a minute ago. Jaiden examined his piano before he sat down. He placed his hands gently above the center of the keyboards, closed his eyes, and played a mellifluous piece. When Kit played the violin, he played with his heart. When he was melancholy, Mina could hear it in his violin. Listening to Jaiden play, Mina had the very same feeling. Mina could tell something troubled him from the way he moved his long fingers fluidly across the keyboard.

Of course he's troubled, Mina! Someone out there wants him dead.

Jaiden continued to play the piano, pouring out his heart through his fingertips, as if the world and time around him had stopped.

Mina stood by the doorway, waiting for Jaiden's next order. She swayed her head as if the music he played mesmerized her.

A minute later, someone knocked on the door. Jaiden opened his eyes and rose from his seat and said, "Come in."

Bunion walked through the door with Madison following behind him. Bunion gave Mina a look that made her want to cower.

"Young Master Jaiden, Miss Helwick is here."

"Thank you, Bunion."

Before Bunion exited the room, he gave Mina an I'm-watching-you glare. Mina returned his look with an apologetic one.

Then she checked out Jaiden's guest, wondering if she was an actress. Miss Helwick wore a white lacey summer dress. Her attractive toes were painted black and white.

Mina scratched the back of her head. *Do I have a problem? I seem to like nice feet.*

Madison approached Jaiden and gave him a peck on the right cheek.

"Good morning, Jai-Jai. I've been dying to hear you play again." Madison batted her eyes. She glanced over at Mina and puckered her brow.

"Why is your maid just standing there, Jai-Jai? I'm parched." Madison licked her upper lip.

"What would you like to drink, Miss Helwick?" Mina asked, a la perfect maid mode.

Madison fanned her face. "Chilled pomegranate juice, please. Five ice cubes."

Do the cubes have to be perfect squares too? Crap. Nodding, Mina asked, "Okay. Would you like something to drink too, Boss?"

"No thank you. After you bring back the drink, you can go vacuum my room. I'll summon you again when I need you."

"Okay."

The minute Mina left the room, Madison chuckled. "Your maid looks funny. She even waddles a bit, don't you think?"

"I didn't notice," Jaiden said.

Madison, as a child, waddled, he remembered.

"She's a bit young to be a Daniels maid, don't you think? What is she, thirteen?" Madison tilted her head.

"She's probably around our age." Jaiden smiled and cracked his knuckles. "What do you want me to play?"

"Something fast and lively, so I can dance." She beamed at him.

"You got it." Jaiden closed his eyes and played a jazzed-up version of Mary Had a Little Lamb. Madison wrinkled her brow, chuckled, and danced.

Five minutes later, Mina returned with a frosty glass of freshly squeezed pomegranate juice. Like Jaiden's breakfast, she had the glass on a platter with a silver lid over it. Taking care not to spill the juice, Mina walked over to the pretty socialite dancing. She set the platter down on the coffee table and removed the lid before leaving the privileged couple alone.

A handsome match made in heaven, Mina would admit.

Outside the room, she finally took a breather. Down the hallway stood Bunion waggling his thick forefinger.

"Why didn't you tell me you weren't from the agency, Miss Lin? Thank god my Young Master wasn't upset." He pouted.

"I'm sorry, Bunion. I didn't mean to lie to you." Mina patted Bunion's shoulder. "I hope we can still be friends."

Bunion shot his chin skyward and brushed away her hand. "We weren't friends to begin with. We're also not paid to chit-chat. Please be more professional."

Mina bowed her head. "Right. Sorry about that."

Bunion turned away, head still held high. Mina lugged the vacuum cleaner upstairs to Jaiden's room. First day on the job and she had already royally pissed off her coworker.

~*~

Jaiden took a seat next to Madison on the sofa. They engaged in idle chitchat about the weather and their childhood. Then silence engulfed them. Jaiden tapped his fingers on the sofa and stared at the orchids in the vase.

Madison sipped her glass of juice before she gagged, dropping the glass, spilling dark red juice all over her dress. As sudden as the spill was, Madison's eyes overflowed with tears. She threw herself at Jaiden and hugged him, pressing pomegranate juice onto his light blue shirt.

"What's wrong, Madi?" he asked.

Madison wiped her eyes and sniffled. She hugged him again, almost crushing his ribs. "Promise me you'll help me no matter what, Jai-Jai. Promise me you'll always take care of me."

Jaiden pried Madison's surprisingly strong, skinny arms away from him. He wondered what all these girls were eating that made them so strong.

"Before I promise you anything, I have to know what's wrong

39

first," he said.

"Well… I'm pregnant, Jai-Jai and you're the father of the baby."

"What?" Jaiden didn't even make out with Madi yesterday. Besides, the last time he checked, he was still pristine.

"What I mean is I want you to pretend you're the father of my baby. I want you to marry me."

Jaiden stared at Madison and laughed.

"I'm not joking, Jaiden." She slapped his shoulder. "If you don't help me, Daddy will kill me. You know how Daddy is."

Jaiden touched his temples. Michael Helwick cared more about his reputation and face than Jameson Daniels, threefold. "Who's the real father?"

Madison buried her visage in her hands. "The problem is, I don't know."

Jaiden coughed. "You don't know?"

"I was blitzed at a party last month. You remember how I used to look like, Jai. From an ugly duckling, I turned into a swan." Madison unburied her face. "I loved the way boys finally looked at me. That night at the party, I think I hooked up with at least five guys."

"Five guys? At least?" Jaiden looked away, his eyes stormy. Irresponsible women vexed him. They reminded him of Emma Daniels, the woman who had walked out of his life thirteen years ago. He shook his head to clear the memories.

Jaiden stared at his piano and shook his head. "I really don't think I can help you, Madi."

Madison grunted. "What am I supposed to do then?" Fat tears rolled down the sides of her face. "I swear to you I'm going to kill myself."

Jaiden ran his fingers through his hair, his brow furrowed. Well, he obviously couldn't let her kill herself. Not only would that be irresponsible, it would be the talk of the town. "Let's get you cleaned up first. We'll talk about this later."

Sobbing, Madison said, "Thanks, Jaiden. I knew I could count on you." She kissed Jaiden on the cheek and then trailed kisses down his neck. As good as her kisses felt, Jaiden had no intention of marrying her and being the foster father of her baby. He didn't need someone else's child to suck away his freedom. He pushed Madison away.

"We'll think of something, something that doesn't involve

marriage between you and me. Go upstairs, take a shower, and change." Jaiden walked over to his piano. To Jaiden, as a child Madison was strange and annoying. As a young adult, she seemed semi-psychotic. Jaiden played his piano like the Energizer Bunny on steroids, drowning out Madison's squealing protests with beautiful music.

SIX

Madison stormed upstairs into Jaiden's bedroom, tripping on an extension cord attached to the vacuum cleaner Mina used. Madison cursed and kicked the vacuum cleaner across the room. She kicked the dogs and cats she owned the same way when her mood deemed it necessary for her to physically vent. Violence was in her nature.

"Can I help you with something, Miss Helwick?" Mina stared at the red stains on Madison's dress. At first, she thought Jaiden had stabbed Madison.

I have to stop watching ninja assassin films.

Madison removed her dress and walked into Jaiden's bathroom in nothing but her bra and undies. She was stick-thin, like she had had all her fat sucked out with a lipo-vacuum.

"Start by shutting up and getting me something to change into," Madison snapped.

Unless Jaiden liked to cross-dress, Mina had no idea where to get the princess something to change into. She walked into Jaiden's closet—a space large enough to house four hobos—and rummaged through it, taking out a light pink t-shirt. She left the shirt outside the closed bathroom door.

"I left a shirt for you, Miss Helwick, outside the door."

"I'll call if I need you. You may go."

"Uh, okay." Mina scratched the back of her head. *Am I Miss Helwick's maid or Jaiden Daniels's maid? Jaiden never said anything about me having to serve his girlfriend too.* As Mina finished cleaning the carpet

42

stains, the loud vacuum vroom-sounds hogged her eardrums. Five minutes later, someone tapped Mina's left shoulder.

Mina shut the vacuum and spun around. Madison, wearing Jaiden's pink shirt, stared sabers at Mina. Her dripping wet hair dampened the carpet. She flung her dirtied dress at Mina.

"Why didn't you clean my dress? It's one of a kind, you know? Daddy bought it for me. What kind of a maid is fat and lazy like you?"

Mina opened her mouth to speak. People could call her fat, but how dare the socialite call her lazy. She was about to retaliate before a male's voice filled the bedroom. "Mina's my maid, Madi," Jaiden said, leaning on the doorway of his bedroom and coming to Mina's rescue. She breathed an invisible sigh of relief. "She only listens to me."

What am I, a ping-pong ball? Mina thought. *No, ping-pong balls have more respect than I do,* she thought.

Jaiden closed the distance between him and Mina with long strides. He grabbed her wrist and pulled her toward him. Her hands pressed against his solid chest. Jaiden sent her a fast signal with a wink of his eye.

This will hurt me more than it'll hurt you, Jaiden thought. Without a warning, he bent his head and covered his lips over Mina's. A brief electric shock running from her lips to her toes prevented her from pushing Jaiden away or slapping him. Jaiden wondered if his maid's eyes would be stuck in a permanent state of widened shock.

"Sorry," he mouthed. Mina raised her hand to slap him silly for stealing her first kiss and making her heart run a marathon. He seized her hand before it landed on his cheek. Holding it in the air like a trophy about to slip from his hands, Jaiden faced Madison.

Mina tried to free her hand but failed. She had underestimated Jaiden's strength. That and her heart's violent reaction weakened her.

"Madi-Mina here is actually my girlfriend. She just likes to pretend to be my maid. You know, like with role-playing and stuff." Jaiden hugged his arm around Mina. "She's also pregnant. So you see why I can't really help you, since I can only marry one girl."

"What?" Mina and Madison said in unison. Both dropped their jaws.

Role-play? Do explain! Mina scratched her head.

"Who the hell is she anyway? Jameson is going to be furious." Madison grunted.

"No, my father will be fine with her," Jaiden responded. "And he definitely won't be as furious as Michael, if he knew about you-know-what." Jaiden eyed Madison's belly.

"Slut," Madison screamed at Mina, shoving her roughly as she ran out of the bedroom. Both Mina and Jaiden could hear her screaming from down the hallway, "I hate you, Jaiden Daniels!"

"Ditto," Mina said, wiping her mouth and pointing at Jaiden. "I can sue you for sexual harassment." She berated her heart for thumping.

"Hold that thought." Jaiden walked into his bathroom to brush his teeth for exactly two minutes. He returned to his bedroom with minty fresh breath and zero Mina-germs.

"Fifty-grand," he said.

"Excuse me?" she demanded. "I'll pay you fifty-grand if you pretend to be my pregnant girlfriend."

At first, even Jaiden couldn't believe the words that had just come out of his mouth. For one, Madison was right. Jameson Daniels would dig his own grave if he believed his son had really impregnated a girl like Mina Lin. Jaiden knew he would have to work out some of the kinks later. He analyzed the girl before him.

With a miraculous makeover, she could faintly resemble an heiress or princess from somewhere make-believe.

Happens all the time on TV and in movies, Jaiden mused.

He could technically lie to the world about Mina's identity. Jameson Daniels would accept her if he believed she was someone of importance. Like the Princess of Prunai-Pudai, an unknown island somewhere between Dubai and Brunei. Then, after Madison would stop bothering Jaiden, they would drop the act, pay Mina, and everything would return to normal again.

Jaiden, you're a genius, he thought.

"Me, your pregnant girlfriend?" Mina rubbed her nose. "No way."

"What do you mean, no way? This sort of stuff works all the time in movies and on TV."

Mina arched her brow. *Maybe he should write movie scripts.* "I'm not pretending to be your girlfriend, pregnant or not. Besides, no one would believe we're dating."

And how dare he spoil my good name? Besides, I'll probably be a virgin for life.

Jaiden covered his eyes. "True, but love is blind." He grinned. "Do you know who Madison Helwick is?"

A spoiled, bratty, princess. I know everything about her true personality and nothing about who she is. "Nope." Mina's eyes narrowed into slits. Any smaller and she would fit the stereotype which said that Asians had small eyes.

"She's the daughter of Michael Helwick. CEO of Helwick Incorporated? The Uptown Mayor?" Jaiden's voice held a questioning tone.

"Oh, yea, I know him. Our Penguin Mayor," Mina said.

Jaiden chuckled. "Yes, you are correct."

"Is Madison adopted?" *How could someone so hot pop out of the Mayor?* Mina scratched her head, trying to also analyze the situation before her.

"Nope. Anyway, Madison is so angry because I refused to marry her," Jaiden responded, hoping very much that she would get the background story without him explaining anything.

"So why don't you just marry her? I would, if I were a guy."

Jaiden coughed. "Let's not get carried away discussing your sexuality, Mina. I can't marry her-she's pregnant."

Mina clicked her tongue. "Let me guess. You knocked her up and now you don't want to take responsibility. You suck, you jerk."

Jaiden waved his hands at her. She was calling *him* a jerk? She was the one who was trespassing illegally. He could remind her of that. "No, I didn't knock her up. Would you just let me speak before you hound me again?"

"Okay."

"She hooked up with five random guys at some party, and doesn't even know who the father is," Jaiden said. There. She would get it now, right?

And she called me a slut? "So she wants you to eat the dead cat?" Mina tapped her chin.

"What?" Jaiden expressed, his confusion with his brow wrinkled. The gibberish Mina had blurted, however, curled his lips.

"She wants you to take the blame. You know, like be a scapegoat? Eat the dead cat is a Cantonese saying of the same thing."

"Oh. That's right." He would have rolled his eyes if he hadn't been hopeful. "So you see where you come in, right?"

"You could always tell her you're gay," Mina said.

Jaiden coughed. "You have a problem. I'm friends with a famous psychiatrist-if you need a psych evaluation, please don't hesitate to ask." Who else discussed his sexuality so openly?

"Ha, ha, ha. Don't forget you're asking me for a favor."

Jaiden stretched his neck. "Don't forget you need money. And that you attacked the Comptroller's son earlier. You're also technically still trespassing on private property."

Touché. Mina fisted her hands by her sides. *Unless I can sell both kidneys for twenty-five grand each, and live without them to boot, then I can't lose this job. Who says no to money, anyway? It's not like he's asking me to really be his girlfriend. That would be weird.*

It'll all be pretend, Min. I can do pretend. It would be just like an acting class.

"I'll give you until tomorrow to think about it. You won't regret it-it's just pretend." Jaiden patted Mina's shoulder.

A perfect plan in Jaiden's book in fact-for one, he knew he would never fall in love with his maid, even if he had to spend every waking moment in her presence for the next month or so. She wouldn't fall in love with him either, since she probably liked the fairer sex.

"But until then, you're still my maid." Jaiden put his fisted hand by his mouth as if it were an intercom system. "Clean up in the White Piano Room, please."

Mina rolled her eyes and dragged the vacuum cleaner out of the bedroom, running over Jaiden's feet in the process. She would have done worse to him for stealing her first kiss, had she a pair of scissors handy. It was probably a good thing she didn't.

Jaiden cussed beneath his breath-his crazy maid brought out the worst in him. He looked down at his toes to make sure they were still all intact.

Crazy girls were the bane of his existence. He would bet half of his inheritance a girl had sent him the bloody knife and doll head picture. After all, he had rejected at least a hundred girls ever since he hit puberty, with Madison being Miss Hundred-and-One.

Jaiden walked over and retrieved the plastic bags containing the knife and his smartphone. This wasn't an act of extortion or blackmail. It was a serious death threat aimed at himself and his father. Jaiden picked up the black phone on the nightstand by his bed and dialed Detective Graham's number.

Detective Graham had helped Jaiden on numerous occasions in digging up information regarding his estranged mother. And thanks to Graham, Jameson received juicy facts he used in his smear campaigns against other Comptroller candidates four years ago. He had no doubt that Detective Graham could help him this time.

Jaiden walked down to the basement to check footage from the manse-wide security camera system to see if the person who had left the knife was caught on tape.

Unfortunately, the only two strange people taped were Mina and Mary the real maid. The footage proved neither was the one who had left the knife.

Neither looked good on tape either.

At one part, the tape blacked out for a split second.

Must have been a glitch.

His suspicion growing, Jaiden wrinkled his brow. *Or an insider-job. But who? Bunion? No. Chef? The other maids? Driver?* Jaiden kneaded his throbbing temples before he called his father to warn him about the threats.

~*~

Mina returned home on her bike around six at night with the sun still out and bright. Bone weary ache made her yawn. She stepped into her house and spent the next hour in the kitchen making dinner from ingredients she had stolen/borrowed from the Daniels's kitchen. Once dinner was ready, Mina walked upstairs to her mother's bedroom, assuming Kaila was taking a late-noon nap.

She knocked on Kaila's bedroom door. "Mom, dinner's ready."

No answer. Mina opened the door to find the bedroom empty, the bed unmade, dirty clothes on the floor around the hamper, and the shades drawn.

"When will she learn?" Mina had no doubt in her mind her mother was out gambling again-gambling away the five hundred bucks Mina had given her yesterday.

After stuffing herself with the delicious dinner she had made, Mina climbed up to the rooftop to wait for the sun to set. She looked down and saw Kiterin walking home. Like a puppy excited to see its owner coming home, Mina sat up. About to call out Kit's name, she clamped her mouth shut when she spotted Alyssa waltzing behind Kit.

Mina squeezed her eyes shut. Like an ostrich, she figured if she couldn't see the happy couple, they couldn't see her either. To her dismay, Kit said, "Hey, Min."

"Hey, Mindy!" Alyssa added, her fake smiling showing.

Fire truck. Mina opened her eyes. "Oh, hey, guys. Back from a date?" She planted the most genuine smile that she could muster on her face, knowing that she probably looked like a psycho-tard.

"We just watched a movie and Kit's making me din-din now. Oh, it's so wonderful to have such an *awesome* boyfriend." Alyssa hugged her arms around Kit's torso and smirked. Kit beamed. Mina resisted making a gagging motion.

"Did you eat, Min?" he asked, walking toward his house with his girlfriend's arms still attached around his waist like fat leeches.

"Yes. I even have some food left over if you need any."

"It's okay. Alyssa is very picky." Kit smiled at Mina.

"That's right. You are so good to me, pooki!" Mina wanted to vomit at the scene. They seriously needed to get a room.

"So I'll see you later? Do you want to hang out tomorrow?" Kit scratched his head. "I get off work early."

Mina waved her hand in the air. "No, it's okay. I have to work tomorrow."

"Really? You found a job?" Kit opened the door to his house. Alyssa ran inside, squealing like a happy, sugar-hyper banshee.

Mina had a million things she wanted to tell her best friend. Before she could even tell him one thing, he said, "We'll talk later. I'll call you." He winked and disappeared inside his house, following Alyssa.

Mina arched her neck back, letting gravity pull her tears back into her eyes. Mr. and Mrs. Forrests, Kit's parents, were away on a business trip, leaving Kit alone in the house all summer. The sun disappeared completely, the moon and the stars came out, and mosquitoes pretended to be vampires looming over Mina's carotids.

He's not going to call me. She knew it already. She could have forced herself to believe it in Kit's pre-Alyssa stage, but not now.

Her eyes could crack, she thought, as stared at Kit's house for hours.

I guess Alyssa is sleeping over tonight. No real surprise.

Mina jumped off the roof like a stuntwoman, landing on the grassy lawn with a thud.

Though her ankles felt like they had shattered from the landing, she practiced Mina-Jitsu, perfecting a scissor-air kick. With all her energy focused on martial arts and facing Jaiden's proposal tomorrow, Mina forced her heart not to break.

Not that it could break any more.

Always a fighter, Mina was still not giving up on Kit.

Not yet, at least.

SEVEN

The next morning, Mina arrived at the manse a minute before nine. She wore the same outfit she had worn yesterday. Bunion, with his expression sourer than a lime soaked in vinegar, opened the front door for her. He said nary a word, leading Mina to believe her new boss was still asleep in his bedroom. After not finding him in said room, Mina wandered around the manse until she found him swimming in a man-made waterfall pool by the gardens.

Mina sat by the edge of the pool and splashed water around with her hand to catch Jaiden's attention. Jaiden pulled himself out of the pool, his dark blue swim trunks plastering to his toned thighs. His body glistened and water dripped from his face. He ran his longer fingers through his wet hair and shook his head, water splashing onto Mina.

Mina threw him a white towel she had grabbed from the poolside. He wiped his face and showed Mina how happy he was to see her with a Colgate-Total-worthy smile.

Mina removed a folded sheet of paper from her pant pocket and shoved it at Jaiden's face.

Jaiden motioned for Mina to follow him to the patio table. He wrapped the towel around his body and sat down before he took the paper and unfolded it.

"You wrote a contract?" Jaiden grinned, reading the rough contract his new maid had written, grammar-mistakes, sloppy-script and all.

After practicing Mina-Jitsu, Mina hastily prepared this contract, getting the idea from all the loan contracts Kaila had brought home over the years. Jaiden chuckled as he read the makeshift contract.

I, Jaiden Daniels, will not do anything a guy does to a girl when Mina Lin is posing as his pretend girlfriend. I will pay her $50,000 when her duties are fulfilled. I will not do anything that makes her uncomfortable and will not make her do anything that makes her uncomfortable. I also have to agree that Mina will not really get pregnant. I will sign at the dotted line.

x..

Jaiden cleared his throat. "First of all, not doing anything a guy does to a girl-what about speaking to her? Looking at her? Laughing at her? Emailing her? Please specify. As for doing anything that makes her uncomfortable-that's very subjective, don't you think?" Jaiden tore the contract before Mina's eyes. He knew it would never hold up in court.

"Hey!" Mina gathered the shredded bits of paper and murder shone in her eyes. "I spent all night writing that!" *And thought it was lawyer-material worthy!*

"Before you pummel me, hear me out." *Sheesh. What kind of steroids does she pop?* Jaiden raised his hands in defeat-mode. "Let's draft up a more sensible contract together, okay?" It wasn't the idea that bothered him, he promised himself.

"Fine." She tried not to pout.

Half an hour later, they created a new, "more sensible" contract together.

THE REVISED CONTRACT

1. Mina Lin will pose as Jaiden Daniels's pretend girlfriend for as long as she is needed.

2. During this time, she will not have to do anything romantic with him. As they are not a real couple, they will only have to act loving in the presence of others-this act will only extend to hugging, hand holding, and fake kissing like actors when absolutely necessary. (Pressing the sides of their faces together)

3. If neither party breaches The Contract, and they convince Madison Helwick to leave Jaiden Daniels alone, then Mina will receive $50,000. If the act fails, however, Mina will only receive $5000. If Mina breaches The Contract or tells anyone else (the paparazzi, her friends) about this act, she will receive no compensation whatsoever. She may even have to compensate Jaiden for any psychological, physiological, mental, and physical damage she may cause from breaching the contract.

   x...

   x...

Mina reread the contract, scratched out the last line, before she signed it. She shook Jaiden's hand and realized she had just signed a contract with a handsome devil.

"So, starting today, you're my girlfriend, Mina Lin." Jaiden rested his chin on his hand. "First, you'll have to look the part." Jaiden touched Mina's hair. "This style has to go."

"First of all, I'm your pretend girlfriend. Secondly, I'm not getting a haircut."

"Right. Even my pretend girlfriend has to look the part." Jaiden gave Mina a cocky grin, tilting his head.

"But I like the way I look."

Jaiden waved the Contract in Mina's face before he folded it. "This Contract is legally binding. Breaching it means you get zilch off the bat. If I'm unhappy, then you have to pay me."

Mina sighed. "Who do you think you are; my fairy godmother? I don't want a makeover."

"I'm sorry to say this but you're no Cinderella, Mina."

Mina blew a raspberry. *He's right though. Prince Charming would never fall for someone like me.*

Jaiden chuckled. "Meet me out in the front in half an hour. Wait for me by the car that almost killed you." With that, he threw his wet towel at Mina and walked into the manse.

Stupid brat, Mina thought, staring venom-dipped daggers at Jaiden's sculpted back. *Sheesh—he has muscles I didn't even know existed.*

Forty minutes later, garbed in a lavender short-sleeved collar shirt, black slacks, and his favorite designer shades over his eyes, Jaiden found Mina baking in the sun next to his red Maserati.

"You said half an hour," Mina said, tapping her right foot, arms crossed, and face scrunched.

"The sun's good for you and your cute freckles," he replied.

Mina's cheeks turned rosier. She looked away. "Are you sure you want to go out? You're not afraid of whoever's sending you the threats?"

"Not at all. Besides, She-Hulk will protect me, right?"

Mina grinded her teeth and tried to turn the tables on Jaiden. "When does a girlfriend protect her boyfriend?"

"When she's a pretend girlfriend. Get in," he said. Needless to say, he didn't hold the door open for her.

Mina took her time before she obliged, entering the sports car and buckling her seatbelt.

In less than a minute, Jaiden zoomed out of North Uptown. Mina's legs shook and she grabbed onto the leather seat. Blood, heights, spiders-none of that scared her. Jaiden's crazy driving, however, made her bladder want to cry. She tried not to focus on that and focused instead on just staying alive.

Jaiden rolled down the windows and harsh wind whipped at Mina's hair and face. When he parked in front of a hair salon ten minutes later, the wind had already styled Mina's hair into an impressive afro.

Wobbly, she stepped out of the car and almost hurled out her breakfast. "No wonder you almost ran me over. You drive like a hyper cabbie."

"You were jaywalking." Jaiden tried not to laugh at her new hairstyle. "Let's tame that crazy hair." He ushered Mina into Magic, the only hair salon in South Uptown he frequented.

A simple wash, cut, and blow-dry procedure cost three hundred dollars, not including tip. For Mina's hair, a Magic stylist would charge at least five hundred bucks.

Magic, the owner of the salon, ran over to Jaiden's side the moment that the young billionaire walked through the door. Magic adjusted his thick black-box frames and fuchsia tie. He clapped his hands in announcement of the young billionaire's arrival. "Jaiden, you're here!" he squealed.

"Hey, Magic, meet your biggest challenge." Jaiden pushed Mina toward Magic.

Magic's hazel eyes almost popped out of their sockets, looking at Mina. "She's a lost cause! But Magic loves challenges! Leave her to me." Mina bit her tongue, reminding herself that getting angry at the hairdresser would not be a good idea.

Two hours later, Mina left Magic's salon with redefined curls like a doll's. Her lustrous hair was thick and springy, falling past her shoulders. Mina thought she looked five years older, and she didn't dare touch her wig-like hair.

Jaiden spent the past two hours in the salon getting a facial-his pore-less, flawless face glowed. Mina squinted.

"Did you just get your eyebrows done too?" She arched her brow. "Are you sure you don't just want to tell Madison you're gay? Magic would also be very happy."

Jaiden ran his fingers through his silky hair. "Unlike you, Miss Unibrow, I'm straight. Besides, how else was I supposed to kill two hours?"

Mina narrowed her eyes, knowing exactly what he was implying. "I'm straight too." She touched her crumpled brow and felt some stray hairs. Plucking and waxing scared her-she'd rather break her arms fighting people than have her hair pulled out. She had the utmost respect for women who got Brazilian waxes. "You could have hit the gym, or go for a walk in Middle Park."

"Why walk when I have my Maserati? I don't need to hit the gym-I hardly use the one at home. This body is au naturel."

Mina pretended to gag.

He checked out her new hairdo and smiled. "It's passable. Next, let's get you a new wardrobe."

Mina refused to budge. "I hate shopping."

Jaiden crossed his arms. He hated shopping too; especially shopping for others, but this was a mission. *Mission Almost Impossible*, he thought to himself. "Are you sure you're a girl and not really a guy in disguise?"

"Want me to prove to you I'm a girl?" Mina tugged at her shirt, ready to prove herself if necessary.

"I'd rather not be blinded. Listen, let's just get you the clothes and call it a day."

"Fine." *The guy is paying me to get a makeover. Why not? Besides, I can't wait until Kit sees the new me.*

Mina convinced herself dating Alyssa was only a phase for Kit. Mina still believed she had a sliver of hope in winning her best friend's heart. Her new hairdo and nice clothes would definitely help.

After all, she was only pretending to be Jaiden's girlfriend.

Jaiden drove two blocks down to Fifteenth Avenue, where all the designer boutiques of the Uptown were. He stopped in front of Mungo, the chicest of high fashion boutiques in the city. Through the wide glass windows, one could see a plethora of slim mannequins dressed to impress.

MUNGO

The golden sign in script-font glittered as it reflected the morning sunrays.

Jaiden double-parked his car. "Okay, let's go."

"You're just going to park here like that?" Mina gave Jaiden a funny look. He raised his eyebrow back at her. "Aren't you afraid it'll get towed?" she questioned.

"Of course not. Government officials and their families can park anywhere they want." Jaiden pointed to a silver card he placed on the dashboard. He grinned and hopped out of his car.

Head shaking, Mina walked into Mungo like an impressed and intimidated tourist-she had never dared to even window-shop around Fifteenth Avenue in the past.   She figured people would think she were a shoplifter if she stepped into a designer boutique. The treatment she had received at Trendy Star was nasty enough, and Trendy Star was a boutique for the middle-class.

"Are you lost, Miss?"

Mina turned to face a pretty shop attendant in a light pink

uniform. The attendant stepped into Mina's personal space and stared her down as if Mina were a petty thief.

"I... no." Mina prepared herself to turn around and leave, forgetting for a moment her billionaire boss trailed behind her.

The attendant scowled at her as if this was the last thing she wanted to be doing. "You know, this is *Mungo*. Celebrities shop here. We don't allow loitering or soliciting."

Jaiden walked up to the attendant and smiled. "My girlfriend and I are here to shop, not to loiter or solicit." He removed a shiny onyx credit card from his wallet and handed it to the attendant. "Charge everything she purchases on this card please."

"Alright," the attendant said, taking the card and instantly recognizing it to be a limitless Onyx credit card. The card didn't impress her as much as the Daniels's name—Jaiden Daniels, the youngest and most eligible bachelor in all of the Uptown was shopping at *Mungo*.

She swallowed a lump of pride in her throat, disappearing to the back counter before returning with a smile. Her cheekbones reddened like two small apples.

"What are you looking for in particular, Miss? Mungo has everything from purses, jewelry, shoes, to dresses and jeans."

"First, she's looking for an apology," Jaiden said, planting his arms across his chest.

The attendant bit her bottom lip. Mina guessed she wasn't used to apologizing to people very often. "Of course. I apologize for my rude behavior earlier."

Mina scratched her neck and raised her shoulders in a shrug. She probably would have assumed the same thing. "Apology accepted."

"Next, she'll need a handful of different outfits, party and cocktail dresses-just turn her into a princess." Jaiden grinned at Mina, who felt like she had become Eliza Doolittle overnight. At home, her wardrobe consisted of hand-me-downs from her mother and clothes she had worn since she was eleven. This would certainly be interesting.

"Right away, Mr. Daniels. Please follow me, Miss."

About three hours later, Mina left Mungo with ten orange shopping bags in each arm. She had never tried on so many clothes before: lacy and sparkly cocktail dresses, shimmering party gowns, high heels, five hundred dollar jeans, and hundred dollar leggings with holes. She felt just like a model-a size ten one with large calves and no butt. Leave it to the wealthy to spend hundreds on clothes that looked like rags. The total cost for Mina's wardrobe today: eighteen thousand dollars. The satisfaction of Jaiden watching Mina endure makeover-torture: priceless.

"You looked like you had fun," Jaiden said, wiggling his eyebrows. Jaiden couldn't believe it, and he would never in a million years admit it, but he had more fun shopping with his employee than with Madison.

Mina also would never admit it, but she actually did enjoy herself. Whenever she had looked at her dressed up reflection in the mirror earlier, she had actually felt pretty.

I looked like one of 'em socialites.

Jaiden's cheerful demeanor did a three-sixty when he cursed and bolted toward his car.

"The hell." He circled his car, hands fisting his hair.

Mina looked at Jaiden's completely butchered sports car. All four tires were slashed flat. Glass shards and bits from the smashed windows surrounded the car on the street.

"Told you not to double-park." Mina dropped the shopping bags on the ground and inspected the car. "The person threatening you is also a stalker, Jaiden."

"No really, Sherlock?" Jaiden took out his new smartphone and called Bunion. "Arrange for Driver to take me to Father's office. I also need a tow truck to Twenty-Eight on Fifteenth Avenue."

They waited by the street side for about five minutes before the silver-white limo arrived. Jaiden's gruff-looking, hairy chauffeur exited the limo and opened the door for him.

Driver looked like a wild man. He had brown hair everywhere, bushy eyebrows, and a long beard, just like a lumberjack. Bunion the Butler looked like a bald wrestler. The Daniels had strange looking help, Mina included.

"Let's go," Jaiden said, entering the limo. Driver helped Mina put the shopping bags into the trunk before she took a seat next to Jaiden.

If the limo were taller, it could resemble a lounging area at a club with its leather seating, carpeted flooring, flat-screen TV, and mini-bar to the side. On the ride to the D.L.P. main building, Jaiden brooded in silence, not talking to Mina. He pressed his lips together.

Mina cleared her throat. "Do you have any idea who would do something like this?" she asked.

"A psycho, obviously. Who else would destroy my beautiful baby?"

"What, are you going to cry now?" Mina struggled not to laugh at Jaiden's misery.

Jaiden pouted at her, reminding her of an adolescent boy. "You're not going to sympathize? I had the car modified and completely pimped out. It's one of a kind."

"Ghetto talk really doesn't suit you. Besides, it's nothing your money can't buy again." Mina grinned. Jaiden's expression softened.

"The Stalker is so going to pay for this." Jaiden shook his fist in the air, outraged at the scenario.

"He or she has an official name now? You're finally taking this seriously?" Mina asked him.

Jaiden tilted his head. "I've *been* taking this seriously."

Mina shrugged, not sure whether to believe him or not. "So where are we going again?"

"To my father's office. You ready to meet your future father-in-law?" Jaiden gave Mina a boyish grin and rested his head on his arms behind his neck.

"Excuse me?"

"It's time for you to meet the parents. In my case, you only have to deal with my father." He flashed a grin at her.

"When will I have to meet your mother?" She questioned.

Jaiden looked out the window. "Never." He balled his hands into fists, knuckles whitened.

"She passed away? I'm sorry." Mina guessed that this was a sensitive topic and was more than willing to back off quickly.

"She didn't. But she's dead to me. Let's not talk about her." Jaiden changed the topic, re-reminding Mina about her role and how he had to deal with two psychos: the one sending the threats and the one forcing him into marriage.

Still thinking about Jaiden's reaction when she had mentioned his mother, Mina wondered why he was so upset all of a sudden. Deciding not to snoop, she scratched her face and said, "What if Madison is the culprit?" She tapped her fingers together.

"Anyone can be a suspect. Even you." Jaiden pointed at Mina, eyes unblinking and filled with comical gravity.

Mina rolled her eyes at him yet again. "While someone destroyed your car, I was still inside Mungo playing dress-up like a life-sized Barbie doll. You were there, picking out clothes for me... Does that ring a bell?"

"That reminds me. Before you meet my father, make sure you change into that peach dress we picked out."

"You mean the peach dress you picked out," Mina said. *Lovely.*

"Yup." Jaiden winked at her.

They rode the limo to the D.L.P. corporate building in silence. Mina craned her neck skyward, appreciating the structure of the silver-glassed edifice. The bottom floors were curved upward. The skyscraper's unique structure fascinated Mina.

"Impressive, isn't it? Let's go." Jaiden pulled Mina into the building and brought her in front of the restroom. Mina changed into the peach dress and fixed her hair. She walked out of the restroom, demure with her arms behind her back.

Jaiden tilted his head. The peach summer dress flowed to her ankles. To him, she looked like a naïve princess who lived all her life in a cottage atop a grassy knoll. Girls with freckles, he decided, were extra cute. Even if they weren't exceptionally pretty or beautiful,

He extended his hand.

"Hold my hand. It'll be more convincing that way," he said. "You ready to meet my father?"

Mina took Jaiden's hand with her sweaty one. When he didn't pull away, he surprised her. They rode the elevator, still holding hands.

Should I tell him we didn't have to hold hands until we reach his dad's office? She decided not to risk getting him mad again.

A minute later, the pretend-couple ambled into Jameson Daniels's office after Jaiden knocked on the door.

If Mina hadn't already been inside Jaiden's mansion and limo, the office and its amazing view of the city skyline and Thussan River would have impressed her even more than it did now.

Jameson, in his dark gray suit, sat by his desk, with a phone wedged between his right shoulder and face. He motioned for his son to give him a second before he ended his call. After returning the phone to the receiver, he folded his hands. "Pandemonium down at City Hall-rallies against budget cuts again. A day doesn't pass if Uptowners are completely satisfied." Jameson's eyes shifted from his son to Mina. Mina smiled at the Uptown Comptroller-a handsome middle-aged gentleman who resembled a weathered version of Jaiden. Unlike Jaiden, Jameson's eyes weren't violet-blue-they were a striking dark blue.

Jameson did not smile back at Mina. Jaiden held Mina's hand in the air to make sure his father could see. Jameson's expression hardened.

He signaled for the pair to sit. Jaiden pulled a seat out for Mina, across from Jameson.

Jameson extended his hand for Mina to shake. "Jameson Daniels, Comptroller of the Uptown. And who might you be, Miss?"

"Mina Lin." Mina shook Jameson's hand.

"Mina is from Prunai-Pudai," Jaiden said, lying through his pearly whites. Mina stopped herself from smiling-even a fifth-grader could tell Prunai-Pudai was a made up location.

"I've heard of Brunei and Dubai, but Prunai-Pudai?" Jameson's hearty laughter filled his office. "Madison called me earlier this morning. We had a long talk. A very long talk that cut into my conference meeting time." Jameson stroked his beardless chin.

"She told me you're dating one of our maids. Is Miss Mina here said maid?"

"Well-" Before Jaiden could fabricate his lie further, his father interrupted him.

"Don't tell me that Prunai-Pudai is an unknown island in the middle of the ocean east of here. And that this girl before me is some princess." Jameson laughed again.

Always one step ahead of his son, Jameson reached over and patted Jaiden on his shoulder. "If you don't want to marry Madison, I would understand. Besides, you're still young. We can deal with Madison and Michael without fabricating lies."

Chagrined, Jaiden released Mina's hand. "I'll admit it—Mina is my pretend girlfriend." A sinking feeling grew in Mina. *Does this mean I no longer have to work for Jaiden? If that's the case, then he'll pay me zilch!*

Her body on fire, Mina slammed her palms on Jameson's desk, catching both father and son off guard.

"I'm a pauper, not a princess. But that's not what you two should be discussing here. Mr. Daniels, I'm sure you're aware there's a stalker out there who wants you and your son dead."

"I am well aware of that." Jameson faced his son. "Many people would love to kill me.   Oh and Bunion had told me about the damaged Maserati. My deepest condolences to you, Jaiden."

Jaiden dropped his head, an invisible tear rolling down his cheek. "Thank you, Father."

Mina groaned. "Let's be serious here, guys. I have reason to believe your lives are in great danger. I can protect your son and help him kill two stones with one bird," Mina said, her scanning eyes plastered on Jameson's face.

"You mean kill two birds with one stone." Intrigued and amused, Jameson tilted his head downward. "Please elaborate."

Mina inhaled, her chest rising like a puffin penguin's. "In pretending to be Jaiden's girlfriend, I can help him discourage Madison. Plus, I can protect him because I have a black belt in Mina-Jitsu." Mina karate-chopped the air in front of her.

Jameson chuckled. "Is she serious? Mina-Jitsu?"

"Yes, she's stronger and more capable than she appears. Anyway, I'm sure Madison didn't tell you why she wants me to marry her, right?" Jaiden flashed his brows.

"Please enlighten me." Jameson rested his hands on the desk.

"She's pregnant and doesn't know who the father is. You wouldn't want a bastard as your grandchild," Jaiden explained.

Jameson shook his head. "I see." He sat back, turning his swiveling chair to face the windows. "Does Michael know about this?"

"I don't think so," Jaiden said.

Jameson faced the young couple and tapped his fingers on his desk. "Then go ahead. Continue to pretend to date. However..." Jameson stretched his neck. "Madison also mentioned the maid was pregnant. Are you going to pretend to be pregnant, Miss Mina?"

"I really don't want to," Mina admitted. Jaiden nudged her thigh with his knee. In retaliation, Mina stomped on his foot. Jaiden sucked in his breath to prevent himself from grunting in pain.

"It's better that way, Father. I'll have more of a reason to marry Mina than marry Madison," Jaiden said when he regained his composure.

"I would appreciate it if you do not do anything that may affect my reputation and career." Jameson glared at his son for a second.

"I understand, Father."

Jameson picked up a golden pen and twirled it with his fingers. "This means you will have to make sure Madison doesn't run her mouth to the press. You will not have to pretend you're pregnant, Miss Mina. And there will be no pretend marriage."

"I understand, Mr. Daniels." Mina raised her chin at Jaiden, her eyes smirking.

"Jaiden?" Jameson cleared his throat.

"Capisce." Jaiden gave Mina a *thanks-a lot-look*. "And you don't have to worry about a real pregnancy either, Father."

"Good. Now, as for stalker and the threats–I'll tell you what we'll do. I will hire more guards to patrol the manse. Whenever you go out, Driver will be your chauffeur. I will talk to Commissioner Keller about our situation but tell him not to publicize this." Jameson reached for the phone. "As soon as they're needed, the police will be on the case as well."

Jaiden nodded. "Sounds good to me, Father. Detective Graham should have a full list of suspects for me by the end of the week."

"Excellent. So," Jameson looked at Mina, "I trust you will keep my son safe."

Completely serious, Mina saluted Jameson. "I will guard him with my life if need be."

Both father and son glanced at each other and chortled.

Jameson folded his hands. "Alright then, I have more business to attend to. We'll have dinner tonight."

"Yes, Father."

"It was nice meeting you," Jameson said to Mina.

Mina grinned like a goof, as if she had a crush on the handsome, older gentleman. She left the office, following Jaiden. In the elevator, Jaiden let out a sigh of relief.

"That went relatively well," he said. He raised his palm. "High five?"

Mina obliged, smacking his palm soundly with hers. She would take anything that didn't end up with her pretending to be pregnant.

The ride down thirty floors would have taken less than a minute if the elevator didn't jolt its brakes and black out. The sudden stop launched Mina toward Jaiden, slamming her body against his. The closed, dark space reminded Mina of the grave she had fallen into. If she were alone, she would think about her daddy and sink into sorrow. Jaiden, warm and breathing, reminded her how great it was to be alive, even when one was stuck in a busted elevator.

"Don't worry, we'll be okay," Jaiden said, reassuring Mina by not pushing her away. A flashback of a five-year-old Jaiden played before his eyes. The child huddled in the corner of his dark bedroom. Crying, he covered his ears to keep out the sounds of his parents screaming at each other. Vases and fists flew, the walls almost shattered, and the child wondered what he had done wrong to make Mommy and Daddy mad.

Amelia, a young and beautiful maid, wrapped her arms around Jaiden, the same way Mina hugged her arms around him now. Amelia sang him a lullaby, wiped away his tears, and kissed his forehead.

"I love you," Jaiden said, his voice soft and sad. Amelia was his favorite maid-she resigned two years ago for no apparent reason.

Mina pushed herself away from Jaiden. She could feel her heart beating against her chest.

Did he just say he loves me?

EIGHT

The lights flickered before they lit up again. The elevator resumed its journey downward, as if nothing had happened. Likewise, Jaiden smoothed his shirt out with his hands and stretched his neck. Mina planted herself at least a leg's length away from Jaiden.

"You okay?" Jaiden grinned, snapping out of his sad reverie. "What's wrong with your face? It's tomato red."

Mina gulped, trying to come up with something believable. *I must have heard him wrong. He probably said olive-juice or something like that.* "Nothing. I have thin capillaries and whenever I get scared or excited, they spill blood," she blurted. She hoped he would buy that.

"I see." He grinned at her. The elevator door opened, and Jaiden walked out, leaving Mina in the elevator with her heartbeats calming. He turned around and faced her. "I'll have Driver take you home. You can take the rest of the day off."

"Sounds good to me. Thanks, Boss."

After Mina changed into a pair of jeans and a yellow t-shirt, the dress felt too unnatural on her, they entered the limo parked outside the D.L.P. building.

Twenty minutes later, they arrived in front of Mina's house. Jaiden exited the limo with Mina. He scrutinized the two-floored house and said, "It's quaint." He wondered if Mina ever felt claustrophobic in the tiny house. The front lawn was too small. Even a tiny bichon frise wouldn't be happy running around here.

"Behold, my humble abode. I won't invite you inside. Your precious feet might explode on contact with our dirty carpets. Rich Boys don't belong in this part of town," she drawled, noticing the earlier look of disgust on Jaiden's face when they arrived.

Ignoring Mina's comment, Jaiden said, "This is the house you're trying to save, right?"

"It's my Daddy's house," Mina said. "He worked hard to buy it. He had a lot of dreams for this place."

Had? "So your Dad's no longer here?"

Mina shook her head. She squinted, noticing gray smoke from the second floor window-Kaila's bedroom.

"My god."

The debt collectors must have set the house on fire!

Mina launched herself out the limo and ran into her house. Jaiden, spotting the smoke, followed Mina inside her house, taking out his new smartphone to call for help.

Mina ran up the flight of stairs and kicked her mother's bedroom door open. Kaila, sprawled on the floor next to a bucket of burning charcoal, appeared unconscious. Mina fanned the air in front of her face and coughed.

"Mom!"

Seeing Mina's mother out cold on the floor, Jaiden pulled out his smartphone and called the police.

Mina dropped to Kaila's side and scooped her into her arms. She carried her mother out of the bedroom and placed her on the hallway. She dashed into the bathroom and brought back a wet towel to wipe her mother's face. Jaiden checked Kaila's wrist pulse to see whether she was breathing or not.

"She's still alive. It's a good thing the window was open," Jaiden said.

Mina bit her bottom lip, fighting back tears. She didn't want to talk.

I've already lost Daddy. I can't lose you too, Mom.

To Mina, an eternity passed before the police and EMTs arrived. Two paramedics carried Kaila onto a stretcher. Mina hopped onto the ambulance. Jaiden dismissed Driver and followed Mina.

"What are you doing?" Tears brimmed in her eyes. "Just go home. You don't need to come with me." She wiped her face with the back of her hand.

"I know the best doctors at UMC, Mina. Plus, my father knows the president of the hospital. I can help you." Besides, Jaiden would rather spend the rest of the day at Uptown Medical Center than at the manse. Jameson had given him a mandatory summer reading list, economic and finance tomes Michael had published throughout his career.

Business interested Jaiden, but it did not excite him like the medical field. That, and he couldn't stand back and do nothing when Mina's mother's life was in danger.

Jaiden put his hand on Mina's shoulder. "She should be fine. Her lips and face aren't blue-which means she has enough oxygen in her system."

Squeezing Kaila's hands, Mina exhaled and said, "I hope so." Face pale and spirit defeated, Mina managed a weak smile. "Thanks for coming along, Boss."

Miss Marshmallow has a vulnerable side? Interesting.

"I told you, you won't regret working for me." Jaiden winked.

It was only Day Two working for Rich Boy, but already, Mina felt indebted to him.

~*~

Uptown Medical Center, UMC, in the middle of West Uptown, consisted of five buildings one of which was an eight-story glass hospital. Five years ago, Kaila had taken Mina out of class and rushed her to the emergency room here.

The repetitive beeping sounds from machines that looked like primitive-robots, the bright fluorescent rooms, bustling nurses and doctors, and the antiseptic, alcoholic smells were forever etched into Mina's memories. The dark-blue body bag they had put her father's stiff body inside made the eleven-year-old version of her realize death didn't only happen in the news and movies.

And that bad things happened to really good people.

Five years later, stepping into the hectic emergency room, following the paramedics, Mina shivered. Even after the ER doctor who attended to Kaila told Mina her mother would be fine, Mina fretted, pacing the ER back and forth.

Daddy was perfectly fine the day before he died.

Jaiden pulled the ER doctor aside. He offered the young doctor his hand to shake. "Jaiden Daniels," Jaiden said, eyeing the doctor's

ID. Dr. Wang was a resident, a practicing doctor fresh out of medical school. In a few years, Jaiden hoped to be in this guy's shoes. Jameson, of course, had other plans for Jaiden, all of which involved Jaiden taking over D.L.P. and becoming a politician.

"Please arrange for Dr. D'atria to be Mrs. Lin's attending and transfer her to a VIP suite when she's ready. If this can't be arranged, I'll have my father talk to Wendy," Jaiden said. Everyone in the hospital knew Wendy—she was the president of the hospital.

Dr. Wang adjusted his stethoscope. "Not a problem, I'll make sure everything will be arranged."

"Wait," Mina said, walking toward Jaiden and the doctor. "I can't afford the VIP suite for Mom."

"Don't worry, I'll take care of the hospital bill." Jaiden winked at her again. Mina breathed a sigh of relief.

By five in the afternoon, transporters had taken Kaila to Room 8118, a VIP suite on the eighth floor-a hospital bedroom that looked more like a five-star hotel suite, complete with a spectacular city-view through the ceiling-high windows, a lounging sofa, a flat-screen TV and twenty-four hour room service. Kaila had a private nurse and aide. She slept like a baby, complete with an IV connected to her arm.

Mina, napping on a recliner chair next to her mother, woke up when Kaila stirred in bed. Mina planted herself next to her mother, finally smiling.

When her eyelids fluttered open, Kaila sat up on the plush bed.

"Heaven looks good," she said, touching the soft hospital gown she wore. Her eyes shifted from left to right when she noticed her daughter. "Where's Brian? You're here too, Mina? Oh no, I didn't mean to burn down the entire house."

Mina hugged her arms around her mother, realizing what must have happened. "You're alive, Mom. What were you thinking? Why did you try to commit suicide?" Mina released her mother when Kaila wheezed. Kaila patted her chest.

"Because I'm useless." She put the hospital pillow over her face and sobbed. "I'm pathetic, and I miss your daddy so much. If he could see me now, I know he would be so ashamed."

Mina took the pillow away, and dabbed Kaila's eyes with a pink tissue. Kaila squeezed her daughter's hand, breathed heavily, and her lips quivered.

"I'm sorry for putting you through hell all these years."

Both mother and daughter cried, their tears soaking the one lone pink tissue.

"I was your Daddy's favorite before you were born. I guess I was jealous of you. When he left us, I just couldn't pull myself together. Whenever I gambled, it felt like I had this surge of release, like I don't feel any pain any more, regardless of whether I won or lost."

Mina listened, ecstatic to hear Kaila finally admitting she had a problem.

"So I thought, if I died, then you'll get the house and won't have to worry about paying off my debts. Your dad had purchased life insurance for me too. If I had died, you'd be rich."

Jaiden, standing in silence by the doorframe, had heard everything Kaila had said.

So Mina didn't lie to me, he thought.

"Dying won't solve anything, Mom. And what good is the house and money when I'm all alone?"

More tears rolled down Mina's face, creating two thin rivulets of water flowing down her cheeks. Kaila wiped away Mina's tears with her thumbs, showing genuine love and concern in her dull, brown eyes.

It took a second chance at life to snap Kaila out of her misery. Mina's wait for this day was finally over. Mother and daughter embraced each other, leaving Jaiden feeling warm, fuzzy, and envious.

Jaiden could tell Kaila was a horrible mother like Emma Daniels. Unlike Emma, however, Kaila was willing to grow, change, and learn from her mistakes. Jaiden wondered if he would ever forgive Emma and share a moment with her like the one he witnessed now.

Never.

Emma had left him and had never looked back. She eloped with Jameson's young male intern. According to Detective Graham, Emma and William Wickerham were happily nested away in Australia, living off of Jameson's divorce settlement: a hundred-grand a month.

Five minutes later, Kaila rested on the bed, closing her eyes to sleep again. Mina swept wet bangs away from her mother's face and kissed her on her cheek. She walked to the exit of the room, bumping into Jaiden, not knowing that he had been in the room all along. He wore a white lab coat and a stethoscope on his neck. Earlier, he had disappeared to the hospital cafeteria to get some coffee. Coffee not in hand, he looked just like one of the young residents or medical students roaming the bright hallways.

"You okay?" he asked Mina, looking at her bloodshot eyes and reddened nose and cheeks. When Madison cried, she didn't look half as vulnerable as Mina.

"Peachy." Mina tapped Jaiden's stethoscope. "Thanks again. I really appreciate this. I would have jumped out the window earlier if you weren't here to help out."

"I understand."

"So, you're a doctor now?" Mina grinned.

"I bought these at a supplies store downstairs. It's better to look like one of the medical staff than be recognized as the Comptroller's son. Especially when I have a stalker."

Mina smacked her palm on her forehead. "My god-I would never forgive myself if something had happened to you. I had promised your dad I would protect you."

Mina looked like a disgraced samurai about to perform seppuku. Jaiden stuck his hands into his coat pocket and grinned.

"Don't worry. What could have happened here? Besides, I'm not too worried about the Stalker-nothing he or she has done had hurt me physically-the doll image, the knife, my car." Jaiden shrugged. "Think about it this way-the person probably had plenty of chances to hurt me, but all he or she has done is sent me all these threatening messages."

Mina scratched her head. "What if it's the calm before the storm, you know? Don't treat this lightly, don't brush it off?"

"I'm not treating this lightly, but I refuse to let it bother me too much. Anyway, we should go out and have some fun."

Mina looked at Jaiden as if he had just grown a pair of watermelon-sized breasts. "My mom is sleeping right there. Even though this looks like a hotel suite, we're still inside a hospital. The last thing I'm thinking about now is fun," she admitted.

"How old are you?" Jaiden tapped his chin, as if he was trying to figure it out.

"Sixteen."

"Sixteen? Then how come you act like you're thirty?" She acted older than he did, half of the time.

"What do you mean?" Mina pursed her lips, trying to figure out what he meant. Did he mean that... a horrible thought struck her, "I don't look that old, do I?" she asked.

"You look like you're thirteen, but you act like an adult. Instead of worrying, you should be celebrating." Jaiden waved his hands in the air to demonstrate this point. "Your mom is in good hands; a world famous doctor is attending too her. Plus, she's not on any monitors, which means her vitals are stable." He smiled at her.

"You sound and act like you're a real doctor. How old are you?" she demanded, trying to figure out his age for the first time.

There was one benefit of him pretending to be a doctor: he looked good while doing it. Just like a real Mc. Dreamy or Mc. Steamy, she thought dreamily.

Jaiden played with his stethoscope. She could sense that he looked distinctly uncomfortable with the question. "Eighteen. I guess medicine is my passion. I was a sick kid. I wouldn't be here today if not for Dr. D'atria and medical advances. So you can trust me when I say your mom is in good hands."

"Okay, Boss." Mina couldn't imagine Jaiden as a sick child; he looked perfectly healthy now. He was fit enough to be an athlete. Handsome enough to be a model. *An underwear model.* Mina gasped internally and berated herself for such dirty thought.

"You were really sick as a kid?"

"Yes. When I turned three, I got really sick." He debated internally for a minute before deciding to tell Mina about how he had collapsed face first atop his birthday cake at the age of three, just seconds after he blew out the three candles. Dr. D'atria discovered a plum-sized benign tumor inside Jaiden's head. As a result, Jaiden suffered from seizures and stopped walking. Jameson Daniels had thought his son would be wheelchair bound forever.

Fortunately, under Dr. D'atria's care and supervision, after a successful surgery and a year of physical and occupational rehabilitation, Jaiden celebrated his fourth birthday like any other normal billionaire's child would.

In style.

Though Jaiden had little recollection of what had happened that year, his father had kept photos and videos of everything Jaiden had experienced while he was in the hospital. So even though he didn't remember the original event, he had plenty of memories stored for him of it . Jameson even kept the extracted tumor- freeze-dried in an airless jar for his son.

Creepy, sorta. Cool, hell yes. Other than sports and the news, the only television shows Jaiden currently watched were medical dramas. If his father would allow him to attend medical school, Jaiden had a feeling he would breeze through his courses, thanks to what he had already learned from TV doctors.

At least, that was the theory, anyway.

"That's pretty interesting. And inspiring," Mina said. "Didn't think someone like you would have experienced something like that," she teased, finally smiling.

Mina had a passion too. Actually, she had a few passions. She wanted to be a part-time stuntwoman. As for her main career, she wanted to become an architect like her dad.

"Well, I didn't think you really had to help your mom pay off gambling debts. We're even, then. Okay, let's go de-stress and play tennis in space."

"Tennis in space?" For a second, Mina imagined Jaiden would really take her into outer space to play tennis-just like how astronauts played golf on the moon's surface.

Jaiden just shrugged, not answering her question. "Alright, let's go," he said.

They left the hospital and took a cab ten blocks down to the Astro-Court, a newly built zero-gravity indoor tennis courtyard. Players floated gracefully like trained astronauts as they sent balls spinning across the court. Instead of running to hit the ball, one had to air-swim.

Mina and Jaiden were instructed to change into one-time use space-tennis outfits—white tank tops with loose gray sweatpants.

At first, Mina spun out of control, watching Jaiden play a set with a space-tennis coach like an expert. Jaiden sailed smoothly toward the balls and served them like a pro. Mina dove to retrieve the out-of-bound balls. She could honestly say that she had never had more fun, forgetting her troubles, swimming and dancing like a swan in the air.

"Come join me," Jaiden said. "Just serve the ball like this." He tossed the ball skyward and served it toward Mina. Mina swung at the ball and missed.

She chuckled. "I can't even play real tennis."

"Just try serving the ball," Jaiden offered. Mina tossed the ball into the air, mirroring Jaiden's movements, and smacked it squarely. The ball sliced through the air toward Jaiden. Jaiden sent it right back at Mina, who missed it by inches.

When the set was over, they floated to the Gravity Station and slowly planted their feet on the floor. Mina wiped sweat from her forehead and smiled.

"That was fun." Though she would love to do it again, she knew she wouldn't, at least not on her own. An hour in the Astro Court required annual membership, and the membership fee was five hundred dollars a month.

The rich play tennis. The really rich play space-tennis.

"Next stop, bowling," Jaiden said. Mina frowned at the idea.

"I want to go back to the hospital to check on Mom," she countered.

Jaiden waggled his finger at her. "Remember, we're on a de-stressing mission. You staying in your mom's room and watching her sleep won't do her or you any good anyway."

Though at first Mina resisted the idea, minutes later, they hopped another cab and rode down fifteen blocks to the Neo-Bowl. Mina just couldn't say no to bowling, since it was one of her favorite sports, even though her average was in the mid-sixties. She quickly became the queen of guttering.

Neo-Bowl, however, wasn't a regular bowling alley. The dim alley had longer, wider lanes with human-sized glowing rubber pins. Instead of launching bowling balls down the lane, players launched each other. Mina and Jaiden strapped on their roller-skates with glow-in-the dark wheels.

A live DJ played booming disco music in the background. A waitress on roller-skates served them mango juice and oil-free fast food.

Mina strapped a helmet over her head, and squatted by the end of the lane. Jaiden put his hands around her waist and positioned her for launch. "You ready?" Without waiting for her to answer, he pushed Mina down the lane and she rolled forward, flailing her arms. She knocked over all the pins.

STRIKE! Wobbly, she skated back and gave Jaiden a high five. The gesture seemed natural and practiced, as if they had been friends for a long time. Hanging out with someone other than Kit for a change felt different, but nice.

Besides, Jaiden's not that bad, after all. Now that she knew the real him, she felt much more comfortable with him.

They were done with their activities by nine PM. They returned to UMC. Both were exhausted from playing.

Jaiden stepped into the hospital with Mina trailing behind him.

Call it intuition, call it a nagging feeling. Mina paused and turned around, listening to her gut intuition, which was firmly telling her that something was wrong.

Standing across the street was a slim figure that wore a gray trench coat, gray fedora, and shades. Cover blown, the figure spun around and ran down the street. Instinctively like a predator, Mina bolted after the person. By the time Jaiden turned around to talk to Mina, the suspicious person was gone.

Mina was already halfway down the street across from the hospital, chasing someone in a trench coat like a vigilante.

Give the girl a gun, and she'll shoot before the neurons and synapses in her brain fired. Jaiden shook his head and ran after Mina.

The person Mina chased sprinted fast, like a trained runner. He or she turned a corner, so Mina doubled her pace. Stopping before a dead-end alley, the chased and chaser both panted. Mina studied the person— a woman, she figured. The woman's face was slim and pale.

"You're the Stalker. You sent Jaiden the threatening message, the knife, and busted his car," Mina said, pointing an accusative finger. She readied herself to take down the Stalker.

"I would never do such a thing," the woman said with a soft, soothing voice. She removed her shades and revealed her reflective light blue eyes. With each pretty blink, dark soot lashes fanned her high cheekbones. "I would never do anything to hurt my son."

"Your son?" Mina dropped her fists to her sides. *This is the woman Jaiden had said was dead to him?* Was this really his mother?

With legs longer than a yard each, Jaiden caught up to Mina and the woman.

"Amelia?" Jaiden said, winded and staring at his former favorite maid. "What did you just say?"

NINE

Amelia ran toward Jaiden and embraced his torso, holding him as if he would disappear if she let go of him.

"I missed you so much," she said, weeping openly. She removed her fedora and cascades of dark brown, wavy hair fell past her shoulders.

The woman, who was closer to him than Emma Daniels, was as beautiful as Jaiden remembered her to be. A little thinner and tired looking; but still lovely. She looked very much like Vivien Leigh in her prime.

Not knowing how to react, Jaiden patted Amelia's shoulder. "I missed you too. What did you say before? Something about me being your son?"

Mina did a double take, staring at Jaiden, and then staring at Amelia. Their eyes had the same shape. They had the same nose. Even Amelia's lips, though plumper, also looked similar to Jaiden's. In fact, they looked more like mother and child than Mina did with her mother.

Mixing the shade of blue of Amelia's eyes and Jameson's shade of darker blue, the end result would be Jaiden's violet-blue eyes.

But this doesn't mean she's not a suspect!

"I mean, I love you like you're my son. That's right," Amelia said. "After all, I've watched you grow up."

"I see," Jaiden said dryly before changing the topic. "What are you doing here? Father said you had moved to Japan."

Amelia's eyes darkened at Jaiden's mention of his father. She pressed her lips together. "For the past two years, I've lived in the city."

"Why were you acting so suspiciously?" Mina asked, her arms crossed and her foot tapping. She didn't want to interrupt this sweet moment, but the bodyguard in her couldn't help herself.

"I... I'll admit it. I was following Jaiden. I've been secretly staying in contact with Driver, and I had learned about the stalker's attacks." Amelia faced Jaiden. She touched his cheek. "I just wanted to watch over you and protect you."

Either the woman is a cougar, or she thinks Jaiden is her son. Otherwise, she's being a bit too touchy feely. Mina scrutinized the woman again. She was probably in her early forties, like Kaila. Either that, she thought, *or she's really Jaiden's mother. That would make things very soap-opera-ish,* Mina couldn't help but thinking.

"You don't have to worry about me," Jaiden said. "I'm worried about you, though. Why don't you come back and work for us again?"

Amelia shook her head. "No, dear, I'm retired now. I'm just happy to see you're okay." She smiled sweetly at Jaiden. "I should get going."

Jaiden held onto Amelia's thin wrist. "I'll have Driver take you home."

"I'll be fine. You and your little friend here go ahead and continue with your date."

"We're not dating," Mina and Jaiden echoed in unison.

Amelia grinned and waved her hand. "We'll keep in touch, Jaiden." With that, she walked away, leaving Jaiden staring at her back like a dejected puppy. His legs itched to run after her, but he knew Amelia would just push him away. Two years ago, she had left without saying goodbye.

But as long as she stayed in the Uptown, Jaiden knew he could easily find her. He would start by interrogating Driver. After all, hadn't she said she had talked to Driver?

"You two look related," Mina blurted.

"Yes, people had always said that. My biological mother is a blond haired, green-eyed bitch."

Mina clicked her tongue at him. "Even if that's the case, she's still your mother. She worked hard to bring you into this world. You shouldn't be so disrespectful."

Challenge flashed across Jaiden's darkened eyes. "Your mother didn't abandon you when you were five, did she?"

Mina scanned Jaiden's face. Her demeanor became sullen. "Not physically, but she mentally abandoned me when I was eleven. The same year my Dad left us."

As sad as Jaiden's story was, he had always lived a privileged life—even when he was a child going through rehabilitation. Emma Daniels had abandoned him, but at least she was still alive. And Jameson had provided him with everything money could buy. He forgot that Mina didn't exactly have that.

"I'm sorry." Jaiden looked down at his loafers. "I'll walk you back to the hospital."

Mina shrugged, taking no offence to his hot-tempered statement. "Apology accepted."

One thing he admired about Mina, Jaiden noted, was how easily she forgave people. He patted her poofy hair and grinned at her.

In front of UMC, Mina waited with Jaiden for Driver to pick him up before she went upstairs to see her mother. She spent the entire night on the recliner chair, and she hardly slept at all. Every now and then, she woke up to check if Kaila was breathing properly. Mina had the nurse-bell tied around her wrist. If anything happened, she would be able to call for help. It was in her nature to be a bodyguard; that was probably why she protected Jaiden so well.

Mom…

Though Kaila's forte was tormenting her daughter, Mina knew she would sink into a spiraling depression if she had lost her mother today. Without Kaila, Mina wouldn't have a reason to fight, struggle and force herself to grow up. Losing her father was tough, but because Mina had to take care of Kaila, she didn't have time to be depressed. Mina brushed hair away from her mother's face and fought back tears. She kissed Kaila on the forehead and smiled.

"Love you, Mom."

As usual, Kaila slept like a baby, who wouldn't wake up even if a tornado struck through UMC and brought everyone to the land of Oz.

~*~

The second he stepped into the limo, Jaiden confronted Driver.

"I need a word with you when we're back in the manse," Jaiden said.

Driver turned his face and sneered, much like he always did. "Yes, Young Master."

They returned to the manse and Driver parked the limo. Jaiden exited the vehicle and waited for Driver to come out before he interrogated him.

"So how is dear Amelia these days? Does she like it in Japan?" Jaiden raised his brows.

Driver cleared his throat, sweat beads forming on his forehead. "She really enjoys it there. Especially Tokyo."

"Really? So how come I just bumped into her near UMC?"

Driver scratched his nose. "UMC? Oh right, she did say she was visiting the city in the summer. That's probably why." His expression gave nothing away, however, now that Jaiden knew the truth, he wouldn't hesitate to put pressure on his employee to find out more details.

Jaiden glowered at Driver, letting the man know exactly how he felt about him. "Stop lying. I don't like to have secrets kept from me. You know, plenty of chauffeurs are jobless in the city these days. Most would kill for your position."

Driver turned his face and sneered again. Jaiden could sense the disrespect. "Alright, it's true. Amelia had never left the city."

"Where is she living right now?" Jaiden tapped his foot, waiting for answers.

"Master Jameson wouldn't like it if you went to see her."

"Why not? While we're on this topic, why did she resign all of sudden?"

Driver looked away from Jaiden again.

Jaiden cleared his throat. "We do give nice severance packages, you know."

"Alright, I'll tell you everything. But you will have to promise me you won't tell Master Jameson or anyone else I told you this." Driver held up his hairy right pinky.

"Pinky swear?"

Jaiden didn't have the heart to tell his silly chauffeur a pinky swear had no legal binding value in the courts. He decided to play along anyway, hooking his pinky around Driver's. Driver sucked in a deep breath and told Jaiden everything he wanted to know and more.

Afterward, Jaiden half-regretted forcing Driver to talk. He felt sick to his stomach with this knowledge.

Ignorance is truly bliss after all.

During dinner that night, Jaiden ate his meal in silence. Whenever Jameson asked him a question, Jaiden replied with a shrug, a nod, or a shake of his head. Before their dessert , which was a gold-flaked decadent Swedish-chocolate mousse cake arrived, Jaiden excused himself from the table and retired to his bedroom. He looked out the window and down the room

Downstairs, Driver stood staring directly at Jaiden's bedroom. When he noticed Jaiden, he turned to stare at the moon.

Jaiden frowned and decided to give Detective Graham a call. Driver was seriously creeping Jaiden out.

~*~

The next morning, Mina opened her cracked eyes when sunlight filtered into the room and shone on her eyelids. She yawned and stretched her arms over her head before walking over to her mother's side and checking on her.

Kaila, sitting up in bed, watched the morning news and sipped on a cup of hot coffee. On the nightstand next to her bed rested a big, beautiful bouquet of white roses.

"Good morning, love," Kaila said, putting the cup of coffee on the table tray next to the bed. "So, what secrets have you been keeping from me?" Kaila reached for the bouquet and caressed the soft white rose petals. "Jaiden Daniels, son of our billionaire Comptroller is going out with my daughter? It's hard to believe."

"You've met Jaiden?" Mina looked at the roses, and guessed she had remembered that part.

"He brought the flowers. What a handsome young man. If only I were a decade younger. Don't let go of him, Min-Min."

Mina's eyes rolled. "We're not going out. We're pretending to go out. He's paying me to be his fake girlfriend." Mina took ten minutes to explain everything to Kaila that had happened.

Kaila sipped her coffee again. "So, in a way, you're like a sex-free whore? I see."

"Mom!" Mina's face turned all shades of red and pink. "I'm going through with all of this because of you. How else are we going to pay your debts and save Daddy's house?"

Kaila yawned. "It wouldn't make any sense if you two were really going out. Even though you're my daughter, I have to admit, you're no looker."

"Thanks for the encouragement, Mom," Mina said, sarcasm dripping in her tone. She tried to ignore the hurt as she looked at her mother.

Kaila rubbed her thumb and forefinger together. "So he's our moneybag. Nice."

Mina shook her head. Why was she all about money? "Enough about him. How are you feeling today?"

"Much better. A girl could get used to a place like this."

Mina gave her mother a stern look. "This is the last time in a long time you're ending up in a place like this. It looks glamorous, but don't forget, you're a patient in a hospital."

"I feel good enough to bullfight, love. Now get Mommy out of here. I need to smoke."

Yesterday, Kaila seemed like she had made some progress in rehabbing herself. Today, she regressed, proving the saying "old habits die hard" true.

"You're staying here until the doctor says otherwise." If Mina had to handcuff Kaila to the bedpost, she would. While they were already in the hospital, Mina wondered if she could force her mother to attend a twelve-step rehab program to treat her gambling addiction.

She may as well find out.

"Stay here. I'll be right back, Mom."

"Okie-dokie, darling." Kaila flipped through the TV channels. Mina exited the room and approached the nurse-station in the middle of the hospital floor. She found the bubbly nurse who took care of her mother and tapped the ginger-haired woman on the shoulder.

"Nurse Joy? Is it possible to get my mom some nicotine-patches, and enroll her into free addiction-seminars?"

Nurse Joy smiled at Mina. She had freckles just like Mina, and yet Mina wondered why Nurse Joy looked so much prettier than she herself did.

"That can be arranged. Your mom will just have to sign some paperwork. Then she can come here as an outpatient. I believe Dr. D'atria is discharging her today."

"He is," Jaiden said, striding toward the nurse-station, wearing a pair of baby-blue scrubs. Mina made a face. Nurse Joy grinned and walked toward Kaila's room with nicotine patches.

"What are you, a surgeon today?" Mina asked.

Something about a guy in uniform turned Mina's knees into jelly. She had to admit-Jaiden was one of the cutest guys she had ever met. As a painter, even Kiterin would appreciate Jaiden's looks.

"Actually, I observed an open heart surgery this morning." Jaiden winked. "One wrong cut and the patient would have bled to death." Happy chills ran down Jaiden's spine.

"Okay, well... uh... Anyway, what do I have to do for you today, Boss? If you don't mind, I would like to take the day off to take care of my mom." She hoped that she could get everything arranged in a day.

"You don't have to take the day off, since you and your mom are moving into the manse."

"What? Why?" *The hospital smells must have gotten to his head and made him talk crazy*, Mina thought. Either that or she was dreaming.

"Because that way, we can kill many stones with one bird." Jaiden chuckled. "You and your mother fascinate me, Mina. I want to observe you. If you don't want to live in the manse, then I could come live with you. It could be like a Survivor experience."

"No way," Mina said, face scrunched. "That wasn't part of the Contract." *What am I, an experimental project? He wants to observe me? He's... strange, that's for sure.*

"Well, if you don't stick to me like glue, who will be responsible if the Stalker hunts me down?" Jaiden raised his eyebrows at her. "My life is very precious, you know."

Mina stuck a finger in her mouth, pretending to gag at his tone. "We don't have room for you in our house. We have bedbugs... and our neighborhood is bad." Mina's nose twitched. They didn't have bedbugs, since Mina changed the bedding every other week. Still Jaiden didn't have to know that.

Their neighborhood was much better than the other slums of East Uptown. In the past five years, no one had been killed around her neighborhood. Yes, people had been robbed, mugged, and even run over with by a car. But not murdered. Still this was Uptown and bad things happened everywhere.

Even in North Uptown.

"Then that's exactly why you and your mother are living in the manse."

Jameson Daniels hardly stayed at home, leaving Jaiden alone in a fifty thousand square foot manse often. For now, this was a good thing. Jaiden would rather not see or talk to his father.

As for friends, Jaiden had plenty of them. He had five thousand friends and counting on Facebook, seven thousand friends on MySpace and at least ten thousand followers on Twitter.

Whether they all really cared for him was another story. Sometimes he wondered if he weren't Jameson Daniels's son, would people treat him differently? Would girls like Madison even look at him? Even though he looked otherworldly hot, he knew most females these days cared more about financial stability and power than a man's looks. Especially girls like Madison.

Having real people like Mina and her mother in the manse would definitely liven up the place. Not that Bunion and the other staffers weren't real people, they were, but they were just too formal and robotic. For one, Jaiden felt like he lived in the Eighteenth Century with everyone calling him their Young Master. Plus, they kept secrets from him-big, life altering secrets. He forced away the anger at Driver again.

"Just agree. Think about it this way-treat my manse as a summer getaway. Plus, my staff can keep a close watch on your mom, and make sure she doesn't hurt herself again."

"You do have a point there, Let me think about it." Mina raised a finger to signal for Jaiden to give her a second. She closed her eyes, weighing the pros and cons. Five seconds later, she said, "Alright, we'll move into the manse. Besides, I do owe you. You helped save Mom's life. But I have to take care of some stuff first in our house."

"Great. I'll help your mom with the discharge papers. Driver could take you home."

"Okay."

Half an hour later, Mina arrived before her house in Jaiden's limo. She stepped out of the limo and spotted Alyssa sunbathing in the front lawn in a tiny black bikini. Large shades covered her eyes. She removed them when she noticed Mina.

"A limo? The hell?" Alyssa ran up to study the limo, her breasts almost bouncing out of the small bikini. "Did you win the lottery or something?"

"No."

Mina told Driver to pick her up in half an hour. Driver drove away.

"Sorry, Alyssa, I don't have much time to talk to you." Mina walked up to her front door and reached into her jean pocket for the keys.

"Kit and I had mind blowing sex last night," Alyssa said with a raspy voice.

Mina raised her chin. Her heart felt like someone had squeezed it dry, but she ignored it.

"Congratulations. I hope you guys used protection. Wouldn't want that nice belly of yours to bloat up with a baby," Mina stammered. She had to get out of here before she lost it.

"You don't have to worry about that, I'm on the pill." Alyssa licked her teeth.

"Did you know Kit quit his stupid summer job so he could spend more time with me?"

Mina dropped her keys. "Kit had looked forward to working at LAG all semester long. If you really love him, you would let him do what he wants, and not hog him all summer." *Especially since you're just using him*, she thought.

Alyssa snorted. "Love? I don't love him. He's like a summer fling, honey. Jake's the real deal, but he's away in Europe right now. So, I'll just have to settle for Kit." Alyssa sighed.

Jake Maxbraun, the rich and popular junior jock-football and basketball team captain at Uptown High was Alyssa's "real deal". Mina knew who he was—she had beaten him in arm wrestling.

"Are you serious? You're just toying with Kit's heart?" Mina raised her invisible sleeves, ready to give the flake a good smack down.

"Kit was challenging, but now that's he's mine, I just don't feel challenged anymore. But he'll have to do for the summer."

"What? You bitch!" She was really ready to strike now.

"Nope. That doesn't make me a bitch. This makes me a bitch." Alyssa surprised Mina with a sudden backhand slap across her face, hard enough to possibly snap her jaw.

Mina cocked her fist back, ready to punch in the blond's nose. Alyssa gasped and shielded her face. Kit walked out of his house. Mina quickly brought her fist behind her back.

"What's going on here?" He glared at Mina.

Seeing Kit, Alyssa quickly ran across Mina's lawn to his. She sobbed and pointed at Mina. "I just said something about how much I love you and Mina just went crazy. She wanted to punch me, so I got scared and slapped her."

"Is that true, Min?" Kit looked disgusted. Before giving Mina a chance to speak, explaining the truth of what Alyssa had just said, he added, "What's wrong with you?" He led Alyssa back into his house and slammed the front door.

Exasperated, Mina screamed until her throat bled. She stormed into her house, and cleaned every dusty and dustless surface, just like a maid with an OCD.

"When did I ever hit someone for no reason, Kit? The real question is what's *wrong with you*?" Mina kept replaying the scenario in her head, wishing she could turn back time and redo everything. She would run up to Kit and show him the red slap mark on her face. She would tell him everything Alyssa had said, about Jake and Kit being her boy-toy plaything. She would cry and act dainty to tug at his heartstrings.

"But would he believe me?" Mina screamed again, wanting to punch a hole in the wall. She wished she had ESP, or other sorts of power, so she could do evil things to Alyssa.

Her cheek still stung from Alyssa's slap. Mina opened the freezer door and stuck her head inside it for a minute.

Then she ran upstairs to scrub the toilet, wash her mother's ash-filled bedroom, and threw out the burnt charcoal. Chores made her sweat, but that was okay. Sweating meant forgetting. Forgetting about what had happened.

But not forgiving. This was Alyssa's final strike, Mina decided. She would not forgive her anytime soon.

She grabbed Kaila's loan contract and packed her mother's clothes in a large, busted gray suitcase. By the time she left the house, Driver had been waiting for over an hour in the limo. He tapped his watch and grunted at her.

"Young Master Jaiden is waiting for us, Miss Mina," he said and sighed.

"I'm sorry," she responded.

"What's wrong with your face? Did that sexy girl slap you?" Driver asked.

"Your name is Driver. Not Asker." She did not feel up to answering questions.

Driver's eyes darkened. He flared his nostrils, showing his anger clearly. "Actually, my name is Matt Tirpluc, but everyone tends to forget that. Get in, Miss."

"I'm sorry for being rude, Matt." Mina hopped into the limo, sat back, and refused to cry, squeezing her eyelids shut. Tears, however, still managed to escape.

TEN

Later that afternoon, Jaiden, Mina, and Kaila returned to North Uptown.

"Welcome to my humble abode," Jaiden said as he led a gasping Kaila into his manse. Mina plodded behind them, lugging Kaila's suitcase and looking like a depressed zombie. She had been silent during the limo ride from UMC to the manse. Jaiden had noticed a red mark on her face-her eyes were puffy and red. Like him, she probably didn't sleep much last night. He sensed the issue was about something different, but wasn't sure what.

Jaiden snapped his fingers in front of Mina's face. She didn't flinch.

"What's wrong?" he asked, tapping Mina gently on the forehead. He almost thought her head was hollow when she didn't reply. Mina shrugged, and carried the suitcase up the spiraling staircase.

"She's a space cadet sometimes," Kaila said. "Always in her own little world."

"Your daughter has quite a personality." Jaiden grinned like a rogue. "Sometimes, she's like a firecracker."

"I agree. She takes after her father." Kaila cast her eyes downward, fondly thinking about her husband. He wasn't handsome, but he always knew how to make her laugh.

And he took care of her. He cooked, cleaned, and worked. When he was alive, Kaila remembered that she never had to worry about anything but looking pretty.

The day she married Brian Lin was the happiest day of her life. And the day he left was the darkest.

Kaila smiled and said, "Anyway, I'm so excited to be here. Please show me around your home. It looks like a movie set. Amazing."

"Why thank you, Mrs. Lin. It'll be my pleasure to give you a tour." Jaiden gave Kaila a quick tour of the manse before they bumped into Bunion, who walked out of the kitchen with strawberries in his mouth. Jaiden introduced the two before he left Kaila to Bunion.

"Please show Mrs. Lin around. Take good care of her. She's Mina's mother," Jaiden added.

"Yes, Young Master." Bunion bowed before he froze up like a shy statue in Kaila's presence. His tanned cheeks blushed, and he stammered when he said, "Let me show you the gardens, Mrs. Lin."

"I've always depended on the kindness of strangers," Kaila drawled like Blanche DuBois, hooking her arm around Bunion's muscular one.

Within seconds of meeting the gorgeous lady, Bunion fantasized about her in a white gown walking down a church aisle with doves flying everywhere. Disoriented by his sweet fantasy, Bunion walked straight into the pool, making a large splash. Kaila giggled, slapping her knees and pointing at Bunion's muscular flailing arms, before she jumped right into the pool.

~*~

That night, at a quarter to ten, Mina stared at the phone on the nightstand in her new bedroom-a room larger than the entire first floor of her house. She shared a king-sized waterbed with Kaila. Kaila, after discovering the *non-gambleholic* card games the house staff played nightly in the kitchen, became fast friends with Bunion, Chef, and Head-Maid. If Mina knew her mother had jumped into the pool earlier, a few hours after she had been discharged from the hospital, Mina would forbid Kaila from befriending Bunion.

Mina's hand itched to grab the phone. Her forefinger could dial Kit's number in just seconds.

I have to tell him what had really happened. I have to warn him about

Alyssa.

Mina reached for the phone, dialed the South Uptown area code, before she slammed the phone back down onto the receiver. She couldn't go through with the call.

Forget him, she told herself. So much had happened in the past few days and yet he knew nothing. He wasn't there when she discovered her mother unconscious on the floor. He wasn't there when Jaiden almost ran her over. Where was his shoulder when she cried all those tears?

Despite all of this, she knew she could not erase five accumulated years of love and affection with an emotional purge.

"But you can do it, Min-Min!" To distract herself, she grabbed her mother's loan contract to show to Jaiden. Halfway down the hall toward his bedroom, the entire manse blacked out. A loud thud-sound led Mina creeping along the walls to Jaiden's room.

Asides from sight, every other sense she possessed became heightened. The streaming water down the walls, her soles on the plush carpeting-every sound boomed in her ears. Mina closed her eyes, uncomfortable to see nothing but pitch-blackness with her eyes opened. Her hand reached a doorknob that she assumed belonged to Jaiden's bedroom and shoved open the door.

Jaiden, also lost in the darkness, pulled his bedroom doorknob. One pushed and the other pulled. Mina, strong like a bull during the most inopportune times, pushed the door along with Jaiden. Jaiden stumbled backward, landing on his bottom. Mina walked into the room and tripped over Jaiden's leg. Jaiden's body broke Mina's fall-all one hundred and thirty five pounds of her landed atop him.

"Oof."

They fall to the floor, chest-to-chest, belly-to-belly, and lips to lips.

In the dark, every sensation in their bodies seemed amplified. Jaiden closed his eyes. Mina instinctually puckered her lips, eyes closed again.

Jaiden kissed Mina, pulling her closer to him. His kiss lingered and was filled with urgency and knowing.

The lights flickered and a nanosecond later, the entire manse became well lit again. Mina rolled off of Jaiden and her entire body shuddered. Not from possible cooties she could have gotten from the lip-lock-yes Mina still believed in cooties-but from the way her heart thumped. A pleasant prickling sensation ran across her lips.

He kissed me. That wasn't an accident. Or pretend. He kissed me, hard.

And the worst part about it all—Mina enjoyed the kiss. Despite this, she scrubbed her lips with the back of her hand.

Jaiden sprang to his feet and ran into his bathroom to brush his teeth-three minutes this time and returned to stand next to Mina, ears reddened; from excitement or anger, only he knew.

"What are you doing here at this hour?" he asked, arms crossed and eyes narrowed.

"I wanted to show you something. And I heard a crashing noise," Mina stuttered.

Jaiden pointed at the textbooks scattered by his desk. "I was carrying the books to my desk when the blackout happened." Jaiden didn't tell Mina how the sudden blackout had made him jump and drop all the books. "Thank you for your concern, Super Woman."

Mina glanced at the textbooks-economics and finance mumble jumble.

"You read textbooks at night? And what happened to She-Hulk?" Mina wiggled her brows. Unlike the Hulk, She-Hulk was strong, beautiful, and smart. Jaiden's intended insult was a compliment to her.

Since he acted like the kiss meant nothing to him, she imitated his nonchalance, and waved her mother's loan contract in his face.

"My father runs a multi-billion dollar company, Mina. I'm expected to take over for him when the time comes."

"I thought you wanted to be a doctor."

"Well, even I can't always have what I want," he said.

Mina shook her head. "You should do what you're passionate about. It's your life."

"True. What are you passionate about?" Jaiden's eyes moved from Mina's eyes to her lips. "Fighting? Sabotaging guys to kiss them?"

What? He kissed me! Blushing, Mina stuck out her tongue. "That was a freak accident." His mention of kissing made the pit patting of her heart go crazy. She turned away, her face and neck still hot. "Anyway, I like architecture. One day, I'll be the most famous architect in the Uptown."

Jaiden raised his left brow. "Really? I'd like to see that."

Not giving her a chance to rebuke, he grabbed the loan contract out of her hand and studied it.

"A loan contract?" He scanned the written content, and grinned. "A lot of repercussion for the borrower for mere pocket change." He handed the document back to Mina and walked over to his desk. Sitting down, he reached for a fountain pen and for his checkbook.

"Fifty-grand, coming right up," he said, dotting his Is and crossing his Ts on his signature. He loved saying that he could actually do that. He waved the check. "Here's your payment in advance. But for this, you'll have to accompany me to the charity ball this Saturday and put on a good show. Madison will be there, of course."

That was easy, Mina thought. *A little too easy.*

"There must be a catch… other than just going to the ball with you."

"Well, you'll just have to keep me happy. Otherwise, you'll have to repay me, and I'll slap on a thirty-percent interest rate."

I can do that. Besides, I still have the Contract to protect me if his demands are inappropriate.

Jaiden didn't look like he was joking. Mina took the check and kissed it. "I can keep you happy. Balls, soirees, parties-no problem, Moneybags… I mean Boss. As long as I don't have to dance."

Give Mina a pair of glass slippers, and she'd be dancing on glass shards in no time. During freshman year, she had been in a ballroom dance class. Her partner was a two hundred pound kid who danced with the grace of a weightless ballerina. Mina stomped on his feet during every class, forcing her to drop out of the class and he ended up in a wheelchair.

"You'll have to dance," Jaiden said.

"You'll regret it," Mina replied, fanning her face with the check. First thing tomorrow morning, she would have Kaila send the check to the loan sharks. Then the problem would be over.

Mina walked out of the room. "Thanks for the moola, Boss. Good night!"

Jaiden grinned at her. "You're welcome. Good night." He doubted he knew a person zanier than his newest employee and friend. He admired her unique personality. Although she had violent tendencies and a sailor's mouth, she was simple and real.

All his life, people who wore masks surrounded him-his parents, relatives, and friends. Someone like Mina was a refreshing change; he especially loved the way she overreacted whenever he kissed her. Just to make sure she believed he didn't enjoy their two lip-locking incidents, he brushed his teeth. He remembered how soft her lips were, like sweet rose petals. He just couldn't help himself when she fell on top of him, her lips conveniently atop his. Jaiden grinned.

Just to see her react like a firecracker one more time, he might just have to kiss her again.

ELEVEN

Saturday morning at the crack of dawn, Magic the hair stylist crept into Mina's bedroom in a Michael Jackson-tribute getup, diamond glove and all, with a pair of sharp scissors in his right hand. He inched toward Mina, his footsteps soft like a mouse's, and raised his hand in a stabbing position.

Mina, a light sleeper unlike her snoring mother, opened her eyes and shot up in bed. She felt dazed, like Cinderella on narcotics. Sensing danger, she rolled out of bed and kicked her foot upward, sending the scissor flying out of Magic's hand. Magic flicked his snapped wrist and pouted.

"Magic just wanted to surprise you and give you a makeover in bed!" he explained.

Mina squinted, recognizing the man who had styled her hair earlier in the week. Time had flown. Just last week on the same day, Kit had broken her heart on her birthday, and Kaila had surprised her with a fifty grand debt. The last few days in the manse seemed like a dream-Jaiden's maids catered to every one of Mina and Kaila's needs.

Kaila stayed in the manse, and acted like a privileged socialite. She had caviar for breakfast, bird's nest for dessert, and real shark fin soup with abalone for dinner. Though Mina feared her mother would become spoiled, she was happy Kaila didn't sneak out of the manse to go East Uptown to gamble. Bunion, whose crush on Kaila grew faster than mold on spoiled cheese, left Head-Maid in charge of the manse so he could "babysit" Kaila.

Mina had noticed Bunion had treated her differently lately, and this made her paranoid. Everyone in the manse, except her Jaiden, Jameson, her mother and herself were suspects until the real Stalker was caught.

The Stalker had stopped sending messages ever since he/she trashed Jaiden's car. Despite this, Mina was still on her toes.

Never underestimate the enemy. The Stalker, being in the shadows and silent at present, made things feel eerily like the calm before the storm.

During the past few days, Mina had spent most of her time shooting pool with Chef when she didn't have to accompany Jaiden outside the manse. At night, she practiced Mina-Jitsu in the gardens. Whenever Jaiden left the manse, he went to the D.L.P. building as a summer intern for his father. When they didn't go to the D.L.P. building, he took Mina to West Uptown to play Space-Tennis, skate bowling, and all other types of innovative sports, like underwater golf. Spending all of her time with Jaiden enabled Mina forget about Kit, if only for a little while.

Still, she knew she wasn't attracted to Jaiden in a romantic way. *It's just because I have to protect Jaiden and stuff. And for a spoiled Rich Kid, he's not half that bad.*

Besides, it was fun getting to do things she'd never tried before.

Mina pursed her lips, studying Magic. He probably dressed crazily enough—no offense to him —to possibly be the secret stalker. And there was that whole room-in-the-dark thing. "What are you doing here?" Bra-less in her PJs, Mina covered her arms over her airplane runway chest. "Just because you're gay doesn't mean you can come into my bedroom like this." She narrowed her eyes at Magic. *Yes, even Magic could be a suspect.*

Magic's eyes studied Mina from head to toe. "I appreciate beautiful people and things. You, my friend," he said, snapping his fingers from left to right, "have nothing to worry about." He wrinkled his cute, button nose. "But, after Magic works his magic on you; all of the boys will be drooling."

He winked at her and pulled Mina out of the bedroom.

"What's happening? Why are you working your *magic on me?*" Mina dug her heels into the carpet and refused to budge further in the hallway. She wasn't going anywhere until she was at least dressed properly.

"You have a party to attend tonight, as my lovely Jaiden's partner. He told me to make you the belle of the ball. Which will require some sort of a miracle, but I'm confident in myself." Magic patted his solid chest, perfect pecs formed from daily dedicated visits at the gym. "I am your fairy godmother today, dear, and your godmother won't lie to you. I just can't believe Jaiden would fall for someone like you; the thought boggles my noggin!"

Mina yawned. Insults about her mundane looks no longer fazed her. If people weren't superficial, then supermodels and beautiful actresses would all be unemployed.

"Oh right, *that* charity party. *Fun.* Go ahead; work your magic on me." *Either way, I have no choice but to attend the party. Might as well look good for the night.* Especially since it was likely part of her contract.

After enduring hours of hair straightening and then re-curling, makeup application, and the endless critiquing from Magic, Mina could barely recognize her own reflection when Magic said, "Viola! C'est finit. Magnifique!"

She guessed that meant he had finished transforming her.

Magic had pinned up her hair with elegant diamond barrettes. The airbrush makeup on her face made her skin flawless and her pores invisible. Her cheeks glowed, her fuller lips shone, and her eyes looked larger and anime-ish.

Never in her life had she felt this pretty, or imagined she could look this good. Dangling diamond earrings hung on her earlobes. She wore a simple, but elegant, coral cocktail dress with a diamond studded waist sash. Magic had painted her nails and toes with a similar shade of coral. She wore white heels, and had a matching white clutch.

That evening, walking down the spiraling staircase, Mina felt amazing, at least until she tripped on the last step and flew straight into Jaiden's arms.

"That's it, I'm wearing sneakers to the ball," Mina said, removing herself from Jaiden and standing straight.

"You okay?" he asked. For someone skilled in a weird style of martial arts, Mina was surprisingly klutzy.

Mina nodded and took a quick glance at her always-stylish boss. Jaiden wore a custom tailored black tuxedo, minus a bow tie with the shirt collar unbuttoned. A small diamond stud shone in his left earlobe. The earring did not detract from Jaiden's masculinity—in fact, it gave him an air of mystery and *bad-assery*.

Guys should not look this good. It's just not fair.

Mina looked away before Jaiden thought she was admiring him.

Which I wasn't doing!

He gave Mina a good look and shook his head.

"Something's missing."

For some reason, Mina felt disappointed, she had secretly expected a compliment from Jaiden. *Not for my sake, but for poor Magic's sake—he had put his heart and soul in my look for tonight.*

Jaiden disappeared upstairs, and returned with a black velvet box in his hands. He opened the box, revealing a heart-shaped pink diamond pendant necklace on a white gold chain. Smaller pure white diamonds framed the pink heart. Jaiden dangled the necklace in front of Mina's eyes.

"Perfect," he said after adorning Mina's neck with the sparkling piece of jewelry. The necklace was Emma Daniels's favorite piece. Storming away from her family and the manse, she had forgotten it, and never returned to claim it back.

Mina touched the pendant. *If I sell this thing, I can probably buy ten South Uptown houses or more.* "This must cost a fortune—I can't wear it. What if I lose it tonight?"

"Unless someone yanks it off your neck, it'll stay in place. Besides, after tonight, I'm donating the piece to the charity." Jaiden studied Mina again.

"I'm impressed; you actually look presentable." Presentable wasn't the first word that came to mind when Mina fell into Jaiden's arms earlier. Something funny happened inside of him—as if the butterflies in his stomach had exploded from excitement.

Must have been that tofu taco I ate in the afternoon, Jaiden thought. *Though indigestion wouldn't feel like a happy, fuzzy, and warm feeling.*

"Thanks, though I bet any one could look good when her stylist is Magic and she's wearing a thousand dollar dress." Mina shrugged her bare shoulders.

Magic made a spectacular entrance, using Mina's mentioning of his name as cue, and moonwalked toward Jaiden.

"It was a tough job, but I think I did it. I guess I can finally see why you like her," Magic teased when Mina turned away to admire her reflection in a hallway mirror.

At this rate, I'll turn into a narcissist, Mina thought.

Jaiden prodded Magic in the ribs.

"Hey, that's the thanks I get for taking an impossible job?" Magic pouted and spun around, raising his chin. "That'll be eight-thousand dollars and you're taking me out to dinner, honey." He crossed his arms and tapped his foot.

"It's a deal." Jaiden patted Magic on the shoulder and added with a whisper, "I don't like her."

"Sure you don't, just like how Darcy doesn't like Elizabeth," Magic said, his eyes sparkling. "Have fun tonight, kids! Magic's outta here!" Magic passed Mina in the hallway on his way out of the manse. "Told you all the boys would drool," he mumbled and winked. Mina wrinkled her brow and continued to stare at her reflection, wondering if Kit would choose her instead of Alyssa if he saw her now.

Who am I kidding, anyway?

The day Alyssa had slapped her, Mina already had a makeover. Kit didn't even look at her new hairstyle.

Deep in her unhappy thoughts, Mina didn't notice Jaiden staring at her with intrigue and wonder in his spellbinding eyes.

TWELVE

Thirty-three minutes later, Driver parked the Daniels's silver-white limo in front of Chateau LaPierre, a palace hotel in the upper part of West Uptown complete with its own helipad on the rooftop. Chateau LaPierre was one of the most expensive luxury hotels in the world, receiving six-stars from hospitality industry members throughout the globe. Staying in the grand suites cost ten thousand dollars a night. Renting out the grand ballroom cost well over a hundred grand. Mina often took the train to West Uptown to sketch the Chateau. The exterior of the hotel resembled a large Elizabethan structure, complete with a maze garden, a pool fountain, and live peacocks roaming the vicinity.

The charity ball held in the Chateau raised money for underprivileged citizens of third world countries suffering from summer natural disasters—typhoons, hurricanes, and earthquakes. Everyone who mattered in the Uptown attended the ball through an invitation from the Mayor. Everyone else, especially those who thought they mattered but really didn't, had to purchase tickets for a thousand dollars each to join in on the fun.

Jaiden exited the limo, and opened the door for Mina. Stepping out of the limo, Mina felt like a princess, especially when the flashing camera lights from paparazzi surrounding the Chateau blinded her. Jaiden signaled for Mina to hook her arm around his as he led her up the stone steps in through the golden doors of the hotel. She obliged.

Marble floors lined almost every square-feet of the eight hundred thousand square-foot interior. Large crystal chandeliers hung from the mirror-ceilings. Lush Italian carpeting pampered the soles of everyone's shoes.

Two white tuxedo-clad men stood at the doorway of the main ballroom. A lady in an elegant shimmering aqua dress sat at the reception desk. She recognized Jaiden as she nodded to the men, signaling them to allow Jaiden and his guest entry. They pushed open the doors.

Mina pinched herself, and realized this wasn't a dream. Hundreds of gold and white clothed tables lined the floors, surrounding a dance area that the young ladies from the Regency period would be proud of. The chairs, draped in snow-white cloth, had gold bows wrapped around them. Waitresses and waiters in white suits and black suits navigated the tables with skill.

Jaiden led Mina to the largest table in to the center of the ballroom. Mina recognized a few of the people occupying the table. Michael Helwick looked like the king of penguins in his black tux, white bowtie, and white gloves. Over his bald head, he wore a black top hat. To his left sat his daughter, Madison, in a stunning red gown. To his right sat Jameson, who looked like Clark Gable minus the mustache. Jameson was undeniably handsome, wearing a well-fitted, midnight blue tux. An air of awkwardness hit Mina in the face. Everyone stared at her, especially Madison, who looked like she was ready to commit Carrie-styled homicide.

Jaiden pulled out a chair for Mina to sit right next to Madison. Mina looked down on the seat to make sure Madison hadn't quickly put a vertical-standing needle there. *The last thing I need is a needle in my butt.*

"Everyone, this is Mina, my date for the evening," Jaiden said. "Mina, this is Mayor Helwick. You've met my father and Madison."

Mina smiled at each of them. "Hi," she said.

Madison sneered and stood from her seat. "Excuse me, Jameson, Father. I need a breath of fresh air." She turned to Mina, her nostrils flared. "I guess the Chateau lets just about anyone in these days. Even une grosse vache comme tu." With that, she flipped her long bangs back, and walked away from the table.

Mina didn't need an interpreter to tell her Madison had just insulted her in French.

"I apologize for that, Mina. Madison is still suffering from jetlag, and she had looked forward to attending this ball as a certain someone's date." Michael focused his eyes on Jaiden. Then he smiled at Mina. "Are you of age to vote yet, my dear?"

Mina shook her head. The smile on Michael's face disappeared. "Excuse me, I have to go mingle with some guests. Anyone who can cast a ballot is a friend of Michael Helwick's. I can only say the same for but a few who can't." Michael winked at Jameson and walked toward a group of VIPs.

Jameson folded his hands atop the table and shook his head. "Don't play with fire, Jaiden. This is enough to discourage Madison and Michael." He gave Mina a quick glance and smiled a charming politician's smile. "You look beautiful, tonight."

The compliment brought a blush to Mina's cheeks. "Thank you, Mr. Daniels."

"But don't get used to looking like this or living the life of a socialite. As soon as Madison is back in Paris, this charade is over. Understand?" The sudden sternness on

Jameson's face didn't surprise Mina. Even if she were dressed like a princess, she didn't belong to the Daniels's world.

"I know. To me, this is just a job." Mina smacked her chest like a man full of pride. "Besides, my true purpose here is to protect Jaiden. Just because the Stalker has been quiet, doesn't mean he or she isn't around."

"Father, don't be a spoilsport. Besides, I very much enjoy Mina's company." Jaiden placed his hand on Mina's shoulder. "I might just keep her around even after Madison's gone, and my life is no longer in danger."

"You make me sound like a pet." Mina frowned. After the short exchange, both Daniels were quiet. Tangible tension between them made Mina shift in her seat. She had noticed they hadn't talked to each other much at the manse the past few days. Just like now, they seemed like strangers.

Hor d'oeuvres and refreshments were served, and everyone at the table ate in silence.

Mina wiped her mouth, dabbing it gently like Jaiden did every time after he ate. He ate in small portion sizes, preferring seafood to meats, especially salmon, yellowtail and tuna tartare. If she ate the way he did, she was sure she would lose weight in no time.

Jaiden drank bubbly champagne and conversed with another guest at the table. To occupy time, Mina people-watched and looked around the Chateau.

Kit?

She spotted Kiterin standing alone in a corner of the ballroom. He wore a white formal shirt with a black tie and black slacks. Kit's eyes locked with Mina's from across the room. Recognition did not shine in his green eyes.

My best friend can't even recognize me. Then again, I don't blame him. Regular Mina looks nothing like me now.

Alyssa had mentioned something about attending a charity ball last week, Mina remembered. Even with the distance between them, Mina could sense that Kit felt uncomfortable— underdressed, perhaps and unable to mix and mingle with all the VIPs in the room.

She did not know it, but she had accurately guessed how Kit felt at the moment. He sighed, holding his girlfriend's glass of pink champagne in one hand, and her designer clutch bag in the other. Standing next to him with her back toward him, Alyssa openly flirted with an older guy. The guy wore an eighteen thousand dollar watch, and was supposedly a movie producer.

Tonight, Alyssa's little black dress was too low-cut in the front and the back. Earlier, Kit had offered her his tuxedo jacket to cover up. She had refused. Besides, the AC in the ballroom was a bit too strong and Alyssa had decided not to wear a bra.

Alyssa took Kit's jacket, tossed it on the floor, and stomped on it, complaining about how he should have rented a designer tuxedo like she had told him to, instead of borrowing his father's old mothball smelly one.

Kit would rather sit on the rooftop and stargaze with Mina, instead of spending the rest of the evening here with Alyssa. Thinking about his best friend, he missed her. Mina was loyal like a puppy. As his number one fan, she made him feel like a celebrity.

What comes around goes around, Kit. So this is how it feels like to be played. And yet, he wouldn't dump Alyssa for treating him like dirt. She had him under her spell and wrapped around her pretty finger. Her kisses were like ambrosia to the gods. Her face possessed the golden ratio, and her body was a painter's dream.

"I said I'm thirsty, Kit." Alyssa snapped her fingers. She pouted; upset the movie producer had left her to chitchat with other people who looked like supermodels and celebrities.

Alyssa scanned the ballroom with her heavily made-up eyes. The young gold-digger in her went to work. Her daddy had spent a fortune to buy a ticket to this event.

Kit was like her personal assistant tonight, her wingman.

At age five, Alyssa won third place at a Little Miss Uptown Pageant. At age ten, she knew she could not live without designer bags and shoes. At age sixteen, she was ready to live the life of the rich and famous. Her daddy made a six-figured salary annually, but she knew he couldn't support her for life.

Hence her sole purpose here tonight was to find a sugar daddy.

Or a billionaire bachelor. Then it was to hell with normal guys like Kit, and semi-rich guys like Jake.

"Oh my god, that's Jaiden Daniels!" Alyssa almost squealed. "The tabloids love him—he's like the Prince William of the Uptown." She knew he would be here—the guy of her dreams. Money signs replaced her eyes for a nanosecond.

"Never heard of him," Kit said.

"Of course you've never heard of him, bumpkin."

"I like it when you call me pooki more." Kit chewed the inside of his mouth.

"If you're a good boy, I'll call you pooki all night long at home." Alyssa squeezed Kit's left cheek. "Come along, and let's make friends with our Comptroller and his son."

Mina had kept her eyes on Kit and her heart fluttered when he walked toward their table, following Alyssa. Bubbly, Alyssa sauntered over and waved her hand like a pageant-queen to attract attention. She made eye contact with the Daniels, father and then son. Mina was completely invisible to Alyssa.

Mina kept her eyes on Kit, and even smiled. He looked at her and smiled back, but still didn't recognize her.

"Comptroller Daniels, it's my pleasure to meet you. Thank you for doing so much for our city," Alyssa gushed, offering Jameson her hand to shake. "My name's Alyssa Rabinkaya, I'm studying finance at school and would love to intern for you next summer."

Jameson smiled, his eyes admiring the young woman from head to toe. "It's wonderful to see how young people these days are ambitious." Jameson gave his son a glance. "Unlike others."

Jaiden looked at Mina for sympathy. Mina patted Jaiden's shoulder.

Alyssa nodded and winked. "That's because I have great role models. And this must be Jaiden Daniels, no wonder the tabloids call you the Prince of the Uptown. You're even handsomer in person." She bit her bottom lip. Jaiden, accustomed to all sorts of flatteries and flirtation, grinned and said nothing. Alyssa had the same shade of blond hair like Emma Daniels. The way she moved and spoke reminded Jaiden of that woman. Paying Alyssa no more attention, he turned to Mina and said, "You still hungry, Mina?" He raised his hand to summon a waiter.

Mina shook her head. Kit lifted his eyebrows and did a double take. His eyes widened. Alyssa, finally seeing the girl next to Jaiden as a "love-rival", fixed her eyes on Mina. Never in a million years would Alyssa have imagined Kiterin's frumpy girl next door could end up sitting next to Jaiden Daniels as his date tonight.

"Mina?" Kit said, blinking. "It is you. Wow."

Mina dipped her head coyly and nodded. In the past five years, Kit had never used the expression 'wow' to describe her like so.

"You know them?" Jaiden asked, subconsciously sizing Kit up by subtly sitting straighter.

"No way," Alyssa muttered, frowning. Faster than one could say *fruck*, Alyssa turned her frown upside down and flashed her teeth at Mina. She planted herself behind Mina, and hugged her. "You look amazing, love. Why didn't you tell me and Kit you'd be here? You look just like a big-boned Audrey Hepburn."

Mina pried Alyssa's arms away from her neck and shoulders—if Alyssa showed any more feigned fondness, Mina had a feeling she would be strangled.

"Thanks, but I'm not used to this sort of affection from someone who had slapped me," Mina said, looking at the empty dance floor. She saw an instant opportunity to escape. "Let's get the party started." She took Jaiden's hand and stood, hoping to one-up Alyssa, and make Kit jealous of Jaiden. She prayed Jaiden would play along. Luckily for her, he did.

"Why didn't you tell me you wanted to dance?" He led her to the center of the dance floor. Mina didn't turn her head to look back at Kit when they left the table.

Sorry Jaiden, but you might end up in a wheelchair at the end of the night.

My heels are going to puncture your feet!

Alyssa only just stopped herself from blowing up. She fisted her hands by her sides. Jameson offered her a seat next to him and she obliged. If she couldn't have the younger Daniels, then she would just have to settle for the older one.

Both were the most eligible billionaire bachelors in not just the Uptown, but the entire world. Flirting with Jameson, Alyssa ignored Kit, who didn't seem to mind. He watched Mina move away, and painted a picture of her in his mind. His eyes focused on his ugly duckling best friend, who had turned into a swan worthy to be his new muse.

Meanwhile, on the dance floor, Mina stiffened and held her breath. She inched away when Jaiden placed a hand on her lower back.

"Just relax. Think of dancing as fighting. Step by step, very coordinated and fluid." The past few nights, Jaiden had caught glimpses of Mina practicing martial arts moves in the gardens from his bedroom. Despite her clumsiness, he noticed she could move with balanced ease and agility. To him, she was like a female version of Bruce Lee, strong and full of surprises.

"Just follow my lead." He smiled and took her hand, their fingers entwining. As if on cue, music played in the background, soft and slow, perfect for a romantic dance.

Mina took a deep breath and stepped back as Jaiden took a step forward. The dance floor seemed to melt beneath her feet. Jaiden took a step back and led her to take a step forward. She looked up and saw her reflection in his eyes. He blinked and smiled. "You're doing great. So, what's the deal with the bimbo? She slapped you?"

"Yeah, but I really don't want to talk about it."

"Okay. What about your boyfriend then?" Jaiden shot a glance back at their table and narrowed his eyes at Kit.

"You mean Kit?" Mina looked down at her feet. "Kit's not my boyfriend." She pressed her lips together. "He's my best friend, actually, and Alyssa is his girlfriend."

Jaiden smiled. "Are you happy for them?"

Mina shrugged. "I guess. I mean, they look good together."

"Do you think they're happy together?" Jaiden spun Mina around.

"They should be."

"Then how come the girl keeps hitting on my father, and Kit

keeps staring at you?"

Jaiden could see Mina's face turn red behind the thin layer of foundation she wore.

"Probably because he's still in shock I'm not dressed like a tomboy? What's with all the questions, Jaiden?"

"Just want to know my employee better. Besides, we're friends, right?"

"We are." Mina smiled back. To her surprise, she only stepped on Jaiden's foot once.

They danced another dance before they decided to go to the second floor balcony overlooking the hedge-maze garden. In the center of the maze, Jaiden pointed out, was a knot-garden surrounding a marble statue of a forest nymph and her child.

"Have you ever gone into the maze?" Mina breathed in fresh summer night air. The sun was just about to set. "We should skip the ball, and just run around the maze." It sounded like a preferable option.

"I've navigated the maze before in less than ten minutes. Want to give it a try? I can be your guide." Jaiden offered Mina his hand to hold. Instead of taking his hand, Mina walked over to the edge of the balcony and held the golden rails. The light summer winds hit her face, and stray strands of curly hair danced in the air.

Jaiden tilted his head and felt strong heartbeats against his chest. *Just shut up*, he told his heart. He paced the balcony, visibly uncomfortable as strange feelings rose in him. He stared at Mina again. By their society's standards, she wasn't a beauty. And yet, there was always a spark of life in her exotic eyes. Her face could express a million feelings. When she cried, Jaiden wanted to comfort her. When she was angry, Jaiden shivered. When she was happy, Jaiden just wanted to smile with her.

And tonight, she looked incredible.

Oh god. Jaiden gulped. *Does this mean I...*

Mina sighed. She hoped Kit was jealous of Jaiden. She hoped the way she looked tonight would inspire Kit.

Why am I even still thinking about Kit?

"Yeah, We should skip the party and navigate the maze." Mina smiled and looked down. Blood drained from her face. She jumped backward and cursed.

"Call 911," she said, her lips quivering.

Jaiden looked down over the railing. Like a red rose petal,

Madison lay flat on the ground, two stories down with her red dress fanned, and blood pooling around her.

Jaiden fumbled to retrieve his smartphone and called the police. Ten minutes later, the UPD force arrived and placed the Chateau in complete lockdown mode within half an hour, escorting every guest out of the ballroom. With the charity event canceled, the guests huddled outside around the hotel. Some left, while others stayed to watch EMTs carry Madison into an ambulance. Bloodstained and unconscious, the young beauty was lucky to still be alive after jumping off the balcony.

Michael lost all composure as he entered the ambulance, clutching his daughter's hand. Tomorrow's headlines would all involve Madison Helwick and the Mayor. Everyone would ask the same question: *How could someone continue to run a city like the Uptown if he could not even take care of his own daughter?*

Like a hawk, Driver's eyes scanned the crowd. He pushed through the crowds and put his hand on Jaiden's shoulder. "Let's get out of here, *Young Master*," he said, pulling Jaiden toward the limo and separating him from Mina.

"Wait for Mina," Jaiden said, standing still. Detective Graham had some new information for Jaiden regarding Driver. That information made Jaiden rethink about entering the limo alone with Driver.

Driver frowned. "Don't worry about that silly girl now. Besides, Amelia's is waiting for you."

"Amelia?" Jaiden blinked. *"Amelia is your biological mother. Master Jameson had an affair with her and Emma took you as her own child."*

Mom...

"Yes, Amelia needs you now." Driver pushed Jaiden onward, clasping his hairy hand over Jaiden's shoulder. Jaiden was left with no room to argue.

Jaiden entered the limo and felt faint. A sharp pain in his shoulder made him touch it. He noticed a spot of blood on his fingers and within three seconds, he was out cold.

Laughing like a hyena, Driver locked the doors. By the time Mina realized Jaiden was no longer next to her, Driver had navigated through the crowds and sped down the street.

Before Mina could even register she had been ditched, someone took her wrist and pulled her away from the crowd.

The same person took Mina into his arms and against his chest.

An oaky, familiar scent invaded her nostrils. Every cell in her body reacted. Kit held her in a warm embrace. The chaos around them seemed to dissipate.

"You look so beautiful tonight, Mina. Almost ethereal."

"Thanks." Though she didn't know what ethereal meant, her knees turned jelly-like.

Kit lowered his head and covered his lips over Mina's. His kiss was short and sweet, and yet she didn't feel any fireworks or electricity.

"Come over tonight, Min, please? I'm dying to paint a portrait of you the way you look now. You can be my new muse."

Mina blinked. Her inch long eyelashes fanned her rosy cheekbones. Tonight, she didn't look like Mina Lin. In the expensive dress and makeup worthy to grace the faces of A-listers, she wore a façade and a mask. She felt more confident in herself. *But once the dress is off and the makeup melts, will Kit still want to paint me? And isn't Alyssa his current muse?*

What the hell is going on here?

She commanded her heart stopped beating rapidly.

"Where's Alyssa?" Mina asked, pushing herself away from Kit and looking around. She wiped her lips.

"Somewhere with Jameson Daniels."

Fourteen minutes ago, a police officer had pulled Jameson aside to show him a piece of paper found taped to Madison's dress. Written on the paper was:

Death to those who hurt the Daniels. Only I can hurt them.

Jameson had left with the police to assist in this case, which turned out to be an attempted homicide, instead of a suicide.

Unaware of the seriousness of the situation and feeling unwanted, Alyssa pushed through the crowds, only to find Kit gazing into Mina's eyes—like two lovebirds unaware of the commotion around them. Pent-up frustration could make Alyssa spontaneously combust at any second now.

Both Daniels, father and son, had rejected her advances. The unfruitful night and sudden end to the charity ball made her want to rip out Mina's beautiful curly hair. Instead, she planted herself between the two and said, "I don't mind threesomes. I can share Kit with you, if you share Jaiden Daniels with me."

Mina blinked. "What?"

She shot Kit a glance, and shook her head. "I just saw someone I know flat like a bloody pancake. I can't deal with either of you now."

Mina turned around and Alyssa hissed. She launched her claws at the back of Mina's head, ripping out barrettes and curls. Mina yelped in pain, and jabbed her elbow behind her, right into Alyssa's gut. Alyssa keeled over from the blow, and almost vomited all the champagne and black caviar she had stuffed into her system earlier.

Mina turned around, and stared at Kit. She pulled out the rest of the barrettes that pinned her hair up and tossed them on the ground. She wiped her face, smudging her makeup until she looked like a blitzed clown.

Her fake eyelashes dangled off her real ones.

"This is the real me, Kit, the girl who loved you unconditionally for the last five years. You never wanted to paint her." She blinked and tears rolled out of her gleaming eyes. "I don't think I'll ever stop loving you, but right now, I think you two deserve each other."

For a second, Mina thought she saw remorse in Kit's beautiful green eyes. Then she realized he was probably just confused because she had turned down his offer.

So with that, she walked away from pooki and mooki. Though tears streamed down her face, her lips were U-shaped from ear to ear. In a minute, she wouldn't be smiling anymore, realizing she had to walk all the way back to North Uptown in her heels since she didn't have any cash on her to call a cab or ride the subway. And not even two quarters to make a public phone call to the manse for someone to pick her up. Jaiden had left, and Jameson was nowhere in sight.

Walking in these heels will just make my calves stronger!

This would have been true... if Mina's left heel didn't crack in a pothole halfway back to North Uptown.

THIRTEEN

At eleven-thirty that night, after two hours of trekking across the city in wobbly shoes, of which Mina cracked off the right heel to match the broken left side,, and climbing the North Uptown gates, as they were locked and the booth guard was asleep, Mina returned to Eighteen Richmond Lane to find the manse completely lit, with four police cars parked in the front lawn.

A sudden sinking feeling filled her.

Is someone hurt? Is Mom okay? Mina ran across the lawn to the front door, ignoring the shooting pain in her feet and ankles.

She rang the doorbell and waited outside for less than ten seconds before Jameson, eyes bloodshot, swung open the door.

"Where the hell is my son? You were supposed to protect him!" He pulled Mina into the manse, right before he shook her. Mina shoved Jameson away before he shook her brain out of place. She raised her hands as a sign of pacification.

"Jaiden's not home yet? But he had left with Driver."

"I'm going to kill Matt if anything happens to my son. Why weren't you keeping an eye on Jaiden?"

"I—"

I was too busy dealing with Kit. I was too preoccupied with sorting my own issues.

"I'm sorry," Mina said with her head down.

Jameson screamed, spit landing on Mina's face. Mina turned around when she heard footsteps behind her. She spun around, hoping Jaiden had returned.

"Yelling at her will do nothing, Jameson." A young man in a black t-shirt and ripped blue jeans had appeared through the front door and placed himself between Mina and Jameson.

"Sorry I'm late—got stuck in traffic. But I'm here now, so calm down, James my boy."

"How can I be calm when my son's missing? God, Matt must have plotted this for a while." Jameson ran his fingers through his hair and cursed.

Detective Graham patted Jameson's shoulder. "That's why you should always be nice to your employees."

Jameson glared at Graham. Graham, unfazed, turned to face Mina. He looked at her and smiled, flashing white but semi-crooked teeth. With stubble around his face, his dark blond hair unruly and collar-length, and his eyes a deep gray, the guy looked like an unkempt cowboy. He even had an accent and drawled every sentence. He extended a hand for Mina to shake.

"Detective Graham. You must be Miss Mina Lin. The maid, turned pretend girlfriend, turned bodyguard."

"Uh, yeah." Mina shook the detective's hand. She had imagined him to be much older and a Dick Tracy-type when Jaiden had mentioned he had hired a private detective. Instead, Graham looked as young as Jaiden. Maybe even younger.

"So does this mean Driver, I mean Matt, is the Stalker?" Mina forced herself to remain calm. If anything happened to Jaiden on her watch, she would never forgive herself.

Graham waggled his finger. "The Stalker comprises of three individuals. One is in the UMC ER right now as we speak."

Mina wrinkled her brow. "Madison?"

"Very clever, dear Watson. We'll chat later though. First, let's get rid of the coppers, Jameson. Stop wasting the taxpayers' money. You know I work best solo. Though I can use a sidekick." He grinned at Mina.

"This is Jaiden's life we're talking about. I will not leave my son's life in your hands alone. I trust the police and the Commissioner." Jameson rubbed his temples and looked as if he were about to cry.

To Mina, Jameson had always seemed composed, cold, and calm. He was more like Jaiden's friend and mentor than father. Right now, he acted just like how any normal, worried sick parent would act.

"The police will only hinder things. Everything they do is about legalities and procedures. You wait, and there's a fifty percent chance they will fail. I get the job done, you know it." Graham crossed his arms. "I'll give you a minute to decide, Jameson."

"You sound more like a vigilante than a detective," Mina said. "I agree with Mr. Daniels. The police can help find Jaiden faster. You shouldn't treat this like a game."

Graham didn't respond, but instead arched his brow, glanced at his large black watch, and tapped his foot.

"Fine, I'll do things your way." Jameson rubbed his face and walked away.

Less than five minutes later, all the police left the manse. Jameson returned to tell Graham, "I don't care how much I have to spend. I want Jaiden back home, sleeping soundly in his bed this time tomorrow."

"This is not a good idea." Mina shook her head. "Are you sure you're going to trust a kid?"

"Me, a kid? I'll take that as a compliment. I'm twenty-five in December, Watson."

Mina ignored Graham, and stared at Jameson.

Jameson sighed again before he made his way up the stairs to his bedroom.

Mina became speechless for a minute. "You've got to be kidding. He's leaving you in charge of saving Jaiden alone? Is he crazy?"

"I can cause the entire Uptown to blackout with one mouse-click, Mina. I had provided Jaiden with a list of a thousand suspects, all in in less than a week's time. The list included all three of the Stalkers."

"Madison, Matt, and—"

"Come along with me and I'll tell you, Watson. Even heroes need sidekicks." Graham's eyes scanned Mina's face and then her broken heels. "I'll even give you ten minutes to change, and wash that stuff off your face first." He pulled a fake eyelash away from her eye, and she flinched.

Mina had forgotten that she looked like a drunken clown zombie with her makeup smudged and melted and her hair resembling a bird's nest. And her entire body probably reeked from sweating buckets.

This is not a good idea. Despite her mind reasoning for her to not go along with Graham and Jameson's plan, her feet reacted. She bolted up the stairs, and ran into Jameson in the hallway. He walked toward her and took her hand, placing a black remote in her palm.

"This is a tracking device. Keep it with you. It will help the police follow you and Graham. He's right. They don't know where to start. Matt had left no clues in his apartment, and nothing in the manse." Jameson muttered a curse. "When you find Jaiden, press this button." Jameson pointed at the large round button in the center of the remote. "That will signal to the police to close in." He patted Mina's shoulder. "I'm sorry about what happened earlier, but you can understand how feel, right?"

Mina nodded. "I'll do whatever it takes to save Jaiden."

Jameson closed his eyes. "I will reward you well when you do." He pointed at the necklace she wore. "You can keep that if you save my son."

Mina shook her head and removed the necklace. She handed it to Jameson. Jameson stared at it and thought about his ex-wife. If she were here now, he'd have someone to comfort him.

"It's my fault Jaiden's in danger. I don't need any rewards. Do you think you should come along?" Mina scratched her head.

"I would only hinder things." Jameson shook his head. Jameson did not tell Mina about how he suffered from anxiety attacks and a congenital heart condition. His body could barely take the worry flooding through him.

"You look pale, Mr. Daniels. Will you be okay?"

"Don't worry about me. Just be careful."

Mina nodded again, and watched Jameson disappear into his bedroom. Tonight, even a nightcap would not keep insomnia at bay. For the second time in his life, Jameson prayed. The first time was when he thought that his only son wouldn't grow up.

It took Mina only six minutes to wash her face and change into a pair of jeans, a loose black t-shirt, and sneakers.

She tied her messy hair in a ponytail, and followed Graham out of the manse. Parked three blocks away, Graham's black pickup truck looked like it belonged in a scrap metal junkyard.

"Get in," Graham said, hopping onto his truck and shouted, "Yeehaw!"

Mina hesitated; afraid she would destroy the vehicle with her weight. She climbed onto the passenger seat and buckled her seatbelt.

"You sure you should be driving this? I will remind you that we're going to save someone tonight." Mina had a feeling Jameson couldn't think straight earlier because he was so worried. Other than tag along with Graham, she didn't know what else she could do. At least with the police-tracking device in hand, she had some control of the situation.

"My Baby has never failed me. Besides, she's just twenty-two this year."

Mina cleared her throat. "There's always a first time for everything."

"Nope, not for my Baby." Graham kissed the steering wheel. Instead of revving the engine, Graham turned on his laptop and connected it to a palm-sized satellite-radar.

He rubbed his hands together. "God bless technology. Romeo and Juliet would have lived long enough to become a bickering couple, if they had cell phones."

Mina raised her brows. "Ditto. So, you can find Jaiden with just a touch of a button?"

Graham chuckled. "It's not that simple. Tell me, do you remember if he had his phone with him?"

Mina nodded. "Not the one with the doll's head picture. He had a new one with him."

"Not a problem." Graham's fingers moved on the laptop keyboard so fast, they became a blur.

"Who is the third Stalker?" Mina looked away and closed her eyes. *Please be okay, Jaiden. We're coming to save you.*

"You know Amelia Nool, right?"

Mina blinked. "Jaiden's maid? I knew something was off about that woman when I met her. She even said that Jaiden's her son. I mean they look alike and all, but—"

"She's not his mother. She's wishes she were; she and Matt are together on this, by the way."

While Graham tracked down Jaiden's location, he began to tell Mina everything he had uncovered about Jaiden's three stalkers.

Matt and Amelia had sent the doll head picture and wrapped the bloodied knife in the newspaper, delivering it to Jaiden. Madison was the one who hired some teens to vandalize Jaiden's car after he rejected her. Graham, who learned about what had happened to Madison from Jameson, told Mina how the police had found the note on Madison's dress. He had deduced that Matt was the one who had pushed her off the balcony.

Graham had also revealed to Mina that Amelia was Jameson's secret mistress. Amelia was pregnant with his child, but had a spontaneous abortion five months before the baby was born. Around that time, Emma Daniels was also pregnant. Engulfed with grief, Amelia had developed a mental illness—a serious type of post-traumatic-stress-disorder. She continued her affair with Jameson, and fantasized Jaiden was her child when he was born.

After finally learning about the affair, the year Jaiden turned five, with a heavy heart, Emma Daniels left her family, and had a divorce with Jameson.

Two years ago, Amelia had snapped, and suffered a massive mental breakdown when Jaiden left the Uptown over the summer. Jameson forced her to resign from her position, and had even filed a restraining order against her. Matt, who had always been in love with Amelia, had been vengeful since then.

"I have dug through some health records, and it turns out that Matt has been hiding the fact he has schizophrenia." Graham sighed. "Sometimes, you just don't know who you can trust. And that's why I told Jameson that he should be nice to his employees. Like me. You'd always want someone like me on your team." Graham patted his chest.

Mina tightened her fists around her seatbelt. "That's disturbing. Not your complete lack of modesty, but the part about Matt and Amelia. God, I hope Jaiden is okay." The worry she felt was the same kind of worry she would feel if Kaila or Kit were hurt. She felt sorry for Jaiden. All his life, he had been lied too, and now, he might not even get to know the truth.

No, I can't think like that. We'll be able to save him.

"Hopefully, yes. Alright, I got a location." Graham pointed to a flashing dot on his radar. He pressed the enter button on his laptop and a satellite view of the location appeared on the screen. The image showed a cabin surrounded by evergreen trees. Graham grabbed the steering wheel. "Let's go, Baby."

Baby the pickup truck sounded like it was about to die before it started. Graham stepped on the pedal, hard, and Baby zoomed down the street, almost as fast as Jaiden's Maserati.

"It's all about the nitro." Graham grinned, and almost gave

Mina a heart attack with his total disregard for all traffic laws.

He's worse than Jaiden. Why are all the people around me so over the top?

Mina closed her eyes, praying she wouldn't end up flying out the window before they reached their destination.

We're coming, Jaiden. Please be okay until then. With worry bubbling in her, she now felt the truck didn't seem to go fast enough.

"Step on it, Graham," she said, and Graham obliged, zipping past cars on the Upstate-bound highway.

Meanwhile, back at the manse, Bunion sat before the waterfall pool with a bottle of cognac in his hand. He sobbed.

"If anything happens to my Young Master, I don't know what I'll do." He wiped his eyes.

Kaila strolled into the gardens, and noticed her baldheaded poker-buddy.

"Bun-Bun," she shouted, sauntering over to his side and taking a seat next to him. Without permission, she took the bottle out of his hand, and took guzzle down the cognac before coughing and hiccupping. She laughed, and threw her arms around him.

One thing led to another, and the next morning, they would find their bodies twisted like a pretzel, half their clothes all over the floor of Bunion's bedroom, just like a rated PG-13 plus scene. What they wouldn't know was that they had spent the entire night wrestling. Of course, they would wake up thinking they had done something bad. Hilarity to ensue.

FOURTEEN

Half past midnight, twenty-eight miles away from North Uptown, in a forest cabin nestled in the outskirts of Uptown's Upstate, Jaiden winced and opened his eyes. A sedative that Matt had administered earlier with a hidden syringe in his hand on Jaiden's shoulder had knocked him out. Jaiden's entire body felt weak and achy. With his wrists tied together in a thick, rough rope, Jaiden's fingers grew numb. He looked down. Matt had bound his legs as well.

It was the standard kidnapping scenario, except he was lying on a pile of hay in a giant sized wooden crib. *Chalk one up for creepy.*

"What the hell is going on?" Jaiden demanded as he tried to remove his restraints, tearing the skin around his wrist and ankles. He cursed, analyzing his environment. It was a relatively empty room, with wooden walls and floors, a sole table in the corner with a lit candle, a boarded window, and a closed door. He remained still and closed his eyes so that his hearing would become sharper. He could hear footsteps outside the room.

"Matt! I know you did this. Come out and face me like a man,"

Instead of Matt, the door swung open and Amelia, who was dressed in a white nightgown. She ran into the room, with her arms spread apart.

"My child! You're awake." She smiled, her eyes widened, the shadows beneath them dark and panda-worthy.

"Amelia? Mom?"

"Sweet darling! Yes, I am your mother!" Amelia bit her bottom lip and tears welled up in her eyes. "Finally, you know the truth."

For a second, Jaiden wished he could throw his arms around

Amelia in a warm embrace. Yet, something seemed off about her. For one, she shouldn't be here.

"I'm glad to see you, but why did Matt kidnap me?" he asked.

Amelia reached over the crib to stroke wet bangs away from Jaiden's forehead and face.

"He didn't kidnap you. He merely helped you here. It's so we can do the ceremony later, sweetheart." The way Amelia smiled made the hairs on Jaiden's neck stand erect. She looked at him as if she could look through him, her eyes unblinking and her entire face tensed.

The cogwheels in Jaiden's mind turned. He didn't like the way she had said the word ceremony. He batted his eyes and widened them to achieve puppy-eyes status. "Mom, these ropes hurt me. Could you untie them? Please?"

Amelia tapped her bottom lip with her finger and glanced at the door. "But Matt wouldn't like that, love. I can only loosen them up just a bit so your skin can breathe." She did just that, loosening the rope around his wrists and ankles. With one strong pull, Jaiden assumed he could break loose.

"What kind of ceremony are we doing?" he asked.

Amelia raised her arms. Then she rubbed her belly.

"We're turning back time. Matt says if we do the ceremony, then I'll have my baby back. My poor, poor baby." Amelia blinked and tears rolled down her sunken cheeks. "It will be quick and painless, Jaiden. After that, I'll have one happy family." She blew him a kiss and left the room.

Jaiden shivered. *Death can be quick and painless.*

This Amelia wasn't the Amelia he remembered. With one swift movement, he pulled the rope around his wrists apart. He rubbed his hands as blood rushed back to them. He untied his ankles, shot up to a stand, and jumped out of the crib as if it were a hurdle to a skilled sprinter. He stretched his body, and wondered if he should try kicking the boards covering the window. He was sure Matt was in the next room.

Jaiden reached into his pockets for his smartphone to call the police, only to find it gone.

Obviously Matt had confiscated it earlier and kept it with him. *Crap.*

Jaiden planted his ear by the door and found he could hear Matt's voice. His heart raced, and pumped buckets of adrenaline through his veins. He thought about Mina. If he had her fighting moves and impulsivity, he would just dash out of the room and confront Matt.

Jaiden rubbed his face, and inhaled. His temples pounded, and his body still felt weak from the sedative. The last thing he wanted to do was to hurt Amelia, but by now, he assumed the Stalker comprised of both Amelia and Matt.

From their messages, to what Amelia had just said, Jaiden had every reason to believe his life was in danger. He blew out the candle, and retrieved the metal candleholder before he situated himself behind the door.

"Mother, I'm hungry," he shouted.

"Coming dear," Amelia said. He could hear footsteps. With that, the doorknob turned, and Amelia pushed the door open.

"Jaiden?"

Jaiden jumped out from behind the door, and ran past Amelia. He sprinted out of the room, and wielded the candleholder. Outside the room was the cabin living room. Matt sat, legs crossed, before an unlit fireplace.

Strapped around his chest was a hunting rifle. Seeing Jaiden rush toward him with the weapon, Matt raised the rifle, and aimed it directly at Jaiden's chest. Jaiden hated himself for freezing but he knew if he took another step, he would soon have a bowling ball sized hole in his chest.

"Drop the candlestick, *Young Master*." Matt laughed. "I always felt like a slave working for you Daniels."

Jaiden dropped the candlestick.

"Raise your arms."

Jaiden looked around for an escape, or something he could use against Matt, a weapon of sorts..

"I said raise your arms," Matt screamed. Jaiden raised his arms.

"Shoot him up, Amelia."

Amelia did as she was told, walking over to Jaiden and injecting his neck with a few drops of sedative. Jaiden grimaced. The sedative worked fast, and before he could react, his eyes rolled backward as he dropped to the floor.

"Let's just get this over with. The sooner we perform the ceremony, the sooner your baby will be reborn," Matt said, closing the distance between himself and Amelia. He took her face, in his hands and smiled.

"Alright, let's do it." Amelia knelt down besides Jaiden. She kissed his forehead. "I'm sorry, but after all, you're not really my child. People are selfish. With you gone, my child will be reborn."

Matt prepared a knife by burning it with candle fire. He intended to use the knife to carve out Jaiden's heart. The many voices inside his head had told him this was a magical way to bring back Amelia's baby.

The voices convinced Matt to convince Amelia that a blood letting ritual beneath the full moon an hour after midnight would resurrect her unborn baby. Of course, she would also have to eat Jaiden's fresh heart.

Amelia bent down, and dragged Jaiden out of the cabin.

A quarter of a mile away from the cabin, Baby ran out of gas and Graham cursed. "We'll have to walk the rest of the distance," he said. "The cabin's right up ahead."

"You're kidding, right? How far away from Jaiden are we?"

"About a thousand feet."

Mina hopped out of the pickup truck. "We're not walking there, we're running." She pressed the button on the tracking device. Without a second thought, she ran down the empty roadside. Graham dashed after her. Asthmatic, he ran a hundred feet before he wheezed and stopped.

Lactic acid made Mina's calves burn. Her feet were hurting from the long walk back to the manse earlier. Still, she pushed herself to sprint faster. She didn't care if she busted all her leg joints—Jaiden's life mattered more than her legs.

"Wait, Mina."

Mina stopped running and glared at Graham.

"Do you even know where you're going without the radar? Here, take it. I need to catch my breath." Graham tossed his radar toward Mina and she caught it smoothly like an outfielder.

"Some hero you are. I told you Baby couldn't be trusted," she said before she ran again, following the directions on the radar. She ran like a cheetah on fire, easily covering a quarter mile in less than four minutes.

A million stars lit up the black skies, and she could clearly see. Dozens of fireflies, dreaming of becoming of stars boogied. On such a lovely summer night, heart-carving rituals should not be performed. Try telling that to Amelia and Matt though.

Amelia wiped down Jaiden's body. Her fingers traced the

contours of his face, and his strong jaw-line. She remembered how he reminded her of an owl as a child, with his eyes big, bright, and alert, staring at her in the dark. They were often brimmed with tears when his parents fought.

Amelia always comforted him, pretending he had been born from her womb. Amelia removed Jaiden's tuxedo jacket and shirt. She touched his collarbones and broad chest. His chest rose with each inhale. He looked too beautiful in his sleep to Amelia.

Matt approached Jaiden with the large knife in his hand. He knelt down beside Amelia.

"Ready?" Matt raised the knife, directly over Jaiden's chest.

"Wait. Let me watch him sleep for a little longer. He's so handsome." A soft smile curled Amelia's pale lips.

Matt clenched his teeth. "What? Are you interested in him too? Slut."

When Matt had first learned about the affair Amelia had with Jameson, Matt had wanted to kill his boss.

He had bought a collection of dolls for Amelia. She never appreciated them. Hence, he decapitated all the dolls, and stabbed them every night to vent. He even smeared the doll heads with stray-kitty blood.

Amelia gave Matt an angry look. "Jaiden's my child! I won't let anyone hurt him but me!" Amelia lunged at Matt and grabbed the knife in his hand, slicing her own palms.

She tried to overpower burly Matt, but failed when he shoved her away. She fell backward on her behind.

"I'm killing all the damned Daniels," Matt said, waving the knife at her. "Jameson took you away from me, and now his son is doing the same!" He positioned himself above Jaiden, and raised the knife.

"Jaiden!" Mina arrived in front of the cabin. Before she could even catch her breath, she threw the radar at Matt, hitting him between the eyes. Matt groaned. He stood on the balls of his feet, raised the knife, and ran toward Mina. Mina readied herself and kicked the knife out of Matt's hand, almost shattering Matt's wrist. Mina kicked again, using all of her body's strength, this time aiming at the side of Matt's head. Matt staggered and pointed his finger at Mina.

"I'll kill you too!" Matt launched his fists at Mina. She parried and moved to the side, readying herself to kick again. Her second kick knocked Matt backward.

He fell and his body convulsed before he fainted.

Mina hyperventilated, still breathless from the quarter-mile run toward the cabin. The air she sucked in felt ice cold in her lungs. She wheezed and dropped to the ground next to Jaiden. She patted his face, ecstatic beyond words he was still alive. A strange sensation rushed through her. Relief and joy mixed with another feeling she couldn't decipher.

"Wake up, Jaiden." An eon seemed to pass before Jaiden stirred.

He opened his eyes and felt as if he were Zeus, about to have Athena jump out of his split head.

"Mina." He smiled before his face bore a panicked expression. "Watch out!" He pushed Mina away as Amelia dove at Mina with Matt's knife. Amelia missed stabbing Mina in the back, but thrust the knife into Jaiden's left shoulder instead. Amelia pulled the knife out of Jaiden and blood gushed out of the wound.

"No, no, no!" Amelia dropped the knife and clasped her hands over Jaiden's shoulder. "I'm so sorry! I didn't mean to hurt you. I never did." Amelia looked at her bloodstained hands and wiped them all over her clothes. She buried her face in her hands and wept.

Mina kicked the knife away and knelt beside Jaiden and applied pressure over his wound. "You'll be okay. Just breathe. The police will be here soon."

Jaiden shook his head and reached up to touch Mina's tear stained cheek with his right hand. "You're awesome, you know. I didn't expect you would come to save me." Jaiden coughed. He couldn't even feel the pain in his shoulder anymore—the sedative messed with his brain. His entire body shuddered and the world around him spun.

He closed his eyes and mumbled, "I love you, Mina," before he fainted again.

"Jaiden!"

Arriving just in time to wrap things up, as usual, the police arrested Matt and Amelia. Graham had tagged along in one of the police cars. He hopped out of the car and ran toward Mina and Jaiden.

Minutes later, the paramedics arrived in a helicopter and sped Jaiden back to the UMC. They hooked him up to an IV and a nasal cannula for oxygen. Mina and Graham rode the helicopter with Jaiden. Graham dialed Jameson's number.

"We've rescued your son. He's safe now." Graham snapped his smartphone shut and raised his hand in the air. "High five? Good work, Watson."

Mina narrowed her eyes at Graham and would have punched him in the nose if she had any energy left. "Whatever." She took Jaiden's hand and squeezed it. She could not even register what he had said to her earlier, assuming he had said what he said because he was delusional from his injuries. Everything that had happened seemed surreal.

"It's over now." Mina squeezed Jaiden's hand again, closed her eyes, and prayed.

FIFTEEN

The next morning, Jaiden woke up from a nightmare that left him crying in his sleep. He blinked in his surroundings and realized he was in a UMC private suite. He focused his eyes. Sleeping in a recliner chair next to him was his father. Mina napped on a sofa across from his bed. In sleep, she had her brow wrinkled and under her eyes were dark circles pandas would be proud of. Asleep, Mina still looked imposing and ready to strike down any Stalker, Intruder, or Attacker.

Jaiden flinched when he tried to move his shoulder. Someone had put his left arm in a dark blue sling. Though he had painkillers pumped through his body via an IV, he still felt pain around the knife wound. Unsteady, he got out of bed and Mina woke up.

Without a second thought, Mina limped over to Jaiden and hugged his torso. Her entire body screamed in achy-pain and fatigue. And yet, all the running and fighting was worth it.

"You're okay," she said, fighting back happy tears. Jaiden patted Mina's head with his good hand.

"All thanks to you." Jaiden smiled. "I owe you my life. So I guess I'll have to repay you with my body?" His breathing became heavy. He stared at Mina with fervent eyes. He bent his head and said, "Do you remember what I said to you last night?"

Every pulse in Mina's body thundered. She shook her head.

Jaiden looked at her lips. "I don't know when, how, or why, but I think I love you, Mina."

Mina gulped as her heart pumped a million liters of blood through her body. Not caring he had his father right next to them, Jaiden caressed Mina's cheek with his good hand, closed his eyes and claimed her lips with his. His kiss was soft and slow at first, right before his passion sent fire through her spine to her toes.

For a second, Mina welcomed the dream. Then she pushed herself away.

"You're talking and acting crazy because you're not completely well yet," she said, face red, eyes shifting, and nose twitching.

"I can't explain it. I'm very comfortable when I'm with you... I can be myself," Jaiden said.

"That doesn't mean you're in love with me. This is just a heat of the moment thing. Besides, I don't want to be hurt again." Mina sighed. She hated her lack of confidence, but at least she was realistic.

She coughed, stuttering, "You still have drugs in your system so I'll just pretend what you said and did didn't happen. Sit down before you hurt yourself."

"If I hurt myself, I'll have you to make me better." He admired the sprinkle of freckles across her flushed cheeks. He could see her gulp. He licked his dried lips and looked as if he wanted to crush a kiss to her mouth again.

"You need more rest." Mina forced Jaiden to lie down in bed. "Since you're safe now, you don't need me anymore," she stammered. Seeing Jameson stir as an opportunity to disappear, Mina moved away from the bed.

"You should have a talk with your father," she said, walking out of the bedroom.

You're wrong, Mina, I do need you, Jaiden wanted to say. He sighed and looked at his father. Jameson yawned, stretched his arms over his head and beamed at his son. He looked as if he wanted to hug Jaiden, then hesitated and sat back.

"Last night was hell. The last time I was this worried, you were three years old." Jameson blinked tears from his eyes. Overnight, he seemed decades older to Jaiden. Jaiden sat up in bed.

"I know." Jaiden smiled at his father but the smile quickly faded. "We need to talk. I need to know everything that happened between you, Mom, and Amelia."

Jameson rubbed his tired face and nodded. "I shouldn't have kept any secrets from you. But I was so ashamed of myself." He blinked and tears formed in his eyes. "I'll tell you everything you want to know, son."

Afterward, Jameson apologized to his son. "Because of my mistakes, you lost your mother."

Jaiden, speechless, closed his eyes and laughed as tears rolled down his cheeks. All these years, he had hated Emma Daniels. He had learned everything about her life after she left Jameson. Not once did Jaiden suspect his father, nor did he ask Graham to discover why Emma left.

"I'm sorry, son. I'm sorry." Jameson buried his face in his large hands.

Jaiden blinked away the last of his tears. "Just leave me alone, Father. Give me some time and space to think."

Jameson nodded.

~*~

Outside Jaiden's suite, Mina's heartbeats quieted.

Jaiden's not himself. When he's better, he won't say crazy things again.

Besides, Mina had a feeling that she would win the lottery before a billionaire really fell in love with her.

A minute later, Mina heard wailing and screaming in the adjacent suite. Three nurses and a doctor rushed into the room and the screaming ceased. Mina heard a familiar voice. Curiosity led her to the doorframe. She peeked in and saw Michael pacing in front of the bed. Lying on the bed was a sedated Madison. She had her right leg casted and the top of her head bandaged.

"I don't care what you do. You better make sure my daughter and grandchild are safe." Michael covered his sweaty hand over his eyes. "I don't care how much money I have to spend, as long as they're both okay."

The doctor nodded. "Once the swelling in her brain goes down, Miss Helwick will be fine. As for the leg, she'll be walking normally after approximately six months, as long as she attends regular therapy."

"What about her baby?" Michael grabbed the doctor's white sleeve.

"The baby will be fine."

"Oh thank god." Michael breathed a sigh of relief. "Nothing

matters more to me than my family." He decided he would resign and back out of the Mayoral race. Once his daughter's condition was stable, they would go to Paris and hide away from the public eye. Nowhere else in the entire world were the paparazzi as relentless and cruel as the Uptown paparazzi.

Michael knew they could easily destroy his frail daughter's life. All this, Michael told his sleeping daughter as he stroked her forehead and face.

Mina was glad to see Madison would recover. Perhaps she would learn to appreciate her life more after this ordeal. The accident could really be a mix blessing for her.

Michael's concern and love for his daughter surprised Mina. He even already loved his unborn grandchild. Madison was so sure Michael would have killed her.

Mina smiled, feeling slight envy. *Parents, after all, should love their children. It's just that my own mother is an exception.*

~*~
Earlier that morning

"I will take full responsibility," said the forty-one-years old blushing bald virgin when he woke up in bed next to Kaila. Kaila wrapped her body in a white sheet. She puffed smoke into Bunion's face before she lit another cigarette.

"Responsibility for what? We're adults, aren't we? Besides, I'm sorry but bald men aren't my type."

Kaila's heart would forever belong to her deceased husband. "I don't even remember what happened between us last night."

The truth was, they had shared one kiss and wrestled in Bunion's bedroom like WWF stars before they fell asleep atop his bed. In sleep, they wrestled some more, and ended up with their limbs tangled together.

"We have to get married. I will take care of you and Mina, I promise." Every pore on his body emitted sincerity. Kaila rolled off the bed.

"No means no. Besides, Mina would never accept you as her stepfather. And I like being single." Kaila waved her hand and walked toward the bedroom door. "Poker with the others tonight, right? See you later."

Bunion rubbed his head. Someone had told him if he rubbed

Vitamin E on his head, he would grow some hair. Or he could buy an Elvis-styled toupee. He would have to become buddy-buddies with Mina, buy an engagement ring, and convince Kaila Lin to marry him, for his heart and soul already belonged to the beautiful and bewitching woman. All his life, Bunion had dedicated himself to his work. He graduated Butler Boarding School at the tender age of nineteen and had served the Daniels ever since then, starting with Jameson's father.

Bunion had never thought about love. But now, all he could think about was love.

~*~

That night, Mina returned to the manse after spending the entire day at UMC with Jaiden. Dr. D'atria had estimated he would discharge Jaiden from the hospital on Tuesday. Jaiden had to go through blood tests, MRIs, and X-Rays. Asides from the knife wound, Jaiden had residual sedative in his body, scrapes and rope burn, and a bump in the back of his head. He had hit his head when he fainted the second time.

Everything should be okay. If Madison and her baby could survive the nasty fall, then Jaiden should be fine.

And for some strange reason, when Bunion visited Jaiden today, he had spent most of his time in the hospital making small talk with Mina, asking her what she and her mother liked to eat and do for fun.

It's like everyone has gone nuts. Suddenly, it's like Bunion and I are all buddy-buddy.

Mina made her way to her bedroom. Five minutes later, someone knocked at her door. She regretted opening the door when she saw who her guest was.

Standing outside, wearing shades, a black wife-beater, ripped jeans and worn sneakers, Graham had his hands behind his back.

"Hey, Watson."

"What do you want?"

"I was gonna say goodbye and thank you for your help yesterday."

"Goodbye, and you're welcome." Mina tried to close the door but Graham slipped right into her bedroom. He handed her a bouquet of yellow roses he had kept behind his back.

"For you." He removed his shades. Mina noticed his cheeks turned rosy.

"The hell?" Mina sneezed, pretending to be allergic to roses.

"Well, uh I can't just say thank you without a gift. Besides, Jameson wired a crapload of money into my Swiss bank account. So this is from Sherlock to Watson?" he asked, a question mark in his tone.

"I didn't know they were gay." Mina grinned.

Graham chuckled. "Well, some people are debating if they are. You're feisty. I liked you the moment I met you."

"I thought you were a kook, and I still do. Please just go. I want to go to sleep."

"Me too. I barely slept, thinking about you all night." Graham wiggled his eyebrows.

"Oh, come on. You barely know me."

"Are you sure about that? I'm a private detective. Let's see. You're sixteen years old and—"

"And you're way older than me, so you liking me would make you a pedophile. Thanks for the flowers. See you later." Actually, better never than later, but Mina didn't want to be too rude. "Good night." She shoved him out of her room.

Graham sighed. He whipped out a business card. "Too bad, Watson. You and I could've made one heck of a team. Well, if you ever need me, I'm a phone call away." He winked. "I'll be waiting for your call."

Then you'll have to wait for an eternity. Besides, he almost got Jaiden killed! "Okay, thanks, bye!" Mina slammed her bedroom door shut and plopped down on the waterbed.

Outside, Graham paced the hallway and sighed. "I can wait until you reach a legal age, Mina. I totally can!"

"You're creeping me out, Graham. Good bye."

Graham pouted and walked away.

Mina closed her eyes. Every bone in her body complained, especially her feet. They throbbed and felt detached from her legs. Though her body welcomed sleep, her mind wouldn't stay quiet. Thoughts of Jaiden, Kiterin, and even Graham kept her awake.

Whoever said boys were simple is so wrong. All three boys toyed with her head and her heart. Except Mina had a feeling Graham had a real crush on her. *Of course, the wackiest and least attractive of the trio likes me.*

Her heart had reacted strongly when she thought about Jaiden's kisses and everything he had said to her. She had waited for five years for Kit's kiss and yet when he kissed her, it felt so wrong. But when Jaiden kissed her, it felt so right. All three times felt amazing.

What's wrong with me?

Mina decided she should avoid boys until after college. With the Stalker(s) caught, she convinced herself she had earned the fifty-grand Jaiden had paid her. Madison and Michael would soon leave the Uptown.

Which means Jaiden doesn't need a pretend girlfriend anymore. I could continue to be his maid and bodyguard.

But that would mean I'll spend the rest of the summer in the manse, and run the risk of falling in love again.

Mina-Angel and Mina-Devil appeared on her shoulders, and both reached a similar conclusion.

Because there's no way someone like Jaiden Daniels would ever fall for someone like Mina Lin. And even if he has fallen for me, there's no way he'll love me forever.

In our superficial world, beautiful people belong with other beautiful people. Jaiden may have some feelings for me now because I'm different; odd, strange, violent, but he'll grow tired of me. When I'm deeply in love with him, he'll destroy my heart. My heart will always be the one broken. I can't have that happen again.

One heartbreak was all her heart could take this summer. Before the Pauper fell for the Prince, Mina knew she should leave the manse. For once, she would choose flight over fight. She didn't belong in this ritzy, glamorous world anyway. And before Kaila became delusional, they had to go.

Mina removed herself from the comfy bed and gathered all of Kaila's belongings into the shoddy suitcase she had brought from home.

SIXTEEN

The next morning, Jaiden lay in bed, staring at the door and waiting for Mina to come visit him. Unbeknownst to him, before noon, Mina and her mother were already back in South Uptown in their own house.

He waited the entire day for her visit. His father visited him. Bunion visited him. Mina still didn't show up.

Late in the afternoon the next day, someone he had never expected would visit him came as well.

Emma Daniels walked into the suite with a basket of fruits. She set the basket down on the table next to Jaiden, and looked at her son as if he was a stranger. Both opened their mouths to speak, but neither said a word.

To Jaiden, Emma looked unchanged, as if thirteen years did not pass since he last saw her in person. She was still slim and beautiful, with her blond curls pinned up in a chignon. She wore a pair of tight blue jeans, heels, and a black tank top. Her expression softened when she looked at Jaiden's sling. She turned to face the door.

"Come inside and meet your brother, Aaron."

A blond teenage boy plodded through the door. He removed white ear-buds from his ears, frowned and said, "Hey."

Jaiden laughed, and stared at the boy. "I have a brother?"

Aaron rolled his eyes. He was scrawny, with dark eye circles beneath his light blue eyes. He wore baggy clothes and dog tags around his neck. "A half-brother."

Emma smiled, sat on the bed, and embraced her older son. "I missed you, love. I'm sorry so much has happened and I wasn't here for you. Things will change. I promise." Emma kissed Jaiden's forehead.

"Hey if you're both going to start crying, I'm getting out of here." Aaron plugged the ear-buds back into his ears and blasted his iPod . He sat on the lounging sofa, crossed his legs, and played air guitar with his eyes closed.

Jaiden imagined that they would have great jamming sessions together. Except Aaron would probably think Jaiden was un-cool, since no rock bands included pianists.

"I like him already," Jaiden said, hugging Emma back. "I missed you too, Mom."

Hating someone was draining, and Jaiden was too tired to continue to hate Emma, especially when she had all the reasons in the world to leave his father thirteen years ago.

Jaiden wasn't even mad at his father anymore. After this near death experience, Jameson would allow his son to do whatever he pleased, which included enrolling into medical school next year.

Despite everything that had happened, Jaiden believed he wasn't the biggest victim. Amelia was.

For years to come, Jaiden would watch over Amelia and make sure the people in Epoh, an asylum outside of the Uptown, took good care of her. Every now and then, he would send her white orchids with purple centers, and play her favorite songs at Epoh.

~*~

Wednesday afternoon, Mina sat in front of her house sketching the Daniels's manse from memory. She spent extra time drawing the pillars to perfection.

Inside the house, Kaila played Internet poker. After her brief vacation in the manse, she discovered she loved pai gow, mah jong, poker and the likes for the sheer thrill of mastering both chance and skill gambling games offered. She realized she did not have to gamble away real money to escape from reality. Though she still smoked, drank, and refused to work, at least now she didn't make Mina worry about losing their house.

Mina sighed and looked at their house behind her.

One day, I'll turn this house into the Dream House Daddy had envisioned. I promise, Daddy.

It would take Mina years of practice to be as good as her dad, but she would never give up. Memories of her father would keep her strong for years and years to come.

She knew life wouldn't get any better for them. In September, Mina would have to juggle schoolwork, practicing for the SATs, working to support the family, and running the house again. She was prepared and ready to face all these challenges, but there was one challenge she dreaded.

That was dealing with Kit, who would live next door until he went away for college. Since the charity ball, Mina had not spoken to her ex-best friend.

Speaking of the Devil...

Kit exited his house, wearing a baseball cap, a blue shirt and jeans. He looked at Mina. Mina glanced down at her drawing and ignored him. Her heart did not go crazy. She continued her sketch.

Kit went back into his house and came out again three minutes later. He walked up to Mina and set down a painting next to her.

"I painted this for you."

Mina blinked and looked at the oil painting. Kit had painted her. In the painting, Mina's hair was all over the place. Black rivulets of melted mascara and eyeliner marred her cheeks. Her mouth was open in a scream almost audible.

"When your emotions overflow, you're incredibly beautiful," Kit said, smiling. "I'm sorry I had hurt you, Min." He held out his hand. "Friends?"

Mina touched the oil painting. She had loved every one of Kit's paintings in the past. This one was her new favorite. She nodded and took Kit's hand and shook it. Kit made her stand and pulled her close to him.

"I don't want to lose you again," he said into her ear. "Alyssa was a mistake."

Mina swallowed hard and a rush of sensations hit her like a tidal wave. Yet she wasn't sure this was love anymore.

At the same moment, Bunion parked the silver-white limo in front of Mina's house. He had a black Beatles-styled toupee atop his head (courtesy of Magic). In his pocket was a ring box holding a one-carat diamond ring from Tiffany. He would propose to Kaila for the next sixty days in a row until she would finally say yes on the last day (to everyone's surprise, especially Mina's, but that would be another story, possibly in the sequel.)

Sitting inside the limo, Jaiden stared out the window and saw Kit embracing Mina. Jaiden exited with an air of feigned calmness. His left arm was still in a sling. He walked up to the couple, pulled Mina away from Kit, cocked back his right arm and slammed his fist into the left side of Kit's face.

Kit fell backward from the blow. Mina broke his fall and glowered at Jaiden. She had to prevent a fuming Kit from slugging Jaiden.

"Why did you do that?" she asked, glaring at Jaiden.

Jaiden flared his nostrils. "Why did you leave without saying goodbye?" Hurt filled his violet-blue eyes. "I didn't even get to properly thank you for saving my life."

Mina looked at her sneakers, and her nose twitched. "I had things to take care of."

"Like what?" Jaiden narrowed his eyes.

"You're lucky you're crippled. Otherwise you'd be sorry for touching me," Kit said, spitting out blood. He had never engaged in any violence before, but at this moment, Kit's fists itched to make contact with Jaiden's pretty-boy face.

Jaiden ignored Kiterin. "Come with me," he told Mina, grabbing her left wrist. Kit grabbed Mina's right wrist. The boys pulled her, as if she were an object incapable of feeling or breaking apart.

"Let go of me! What do you guys think I am?" Mina freed herself and ran from the boys.

Who needs boys, anyway?

Mina picked up her pace and turned around. Though she would never admit it, deep in her heart, she knew who she wanted to chase after her. She hoped he could catch up to her.

And he did...

~Fin~

kreamasuzuki.deviantart.com

(…though running after Mina was a bit harder with one arm in a sling.)

Stay tuned for a Maid for Me Sequel, Maid for Me, Too!

Here's a sneak preview of Maid for Me, Too:

MAID FOR ME, TOO

Jaiden Daniels ran after Mina Lin like a madman with an ocean of steroids flowing through his veins. He winced as the pain in his immobilized shoulder intensified. Bearing the maddening pain, he forced himself to catch up to her.

Sprinting quicker, he ignored the gnawing ache in his tired calves. Mina impressed him with her speed and stamina. *How could someone with such short legs run so fast?* Who would even think that she was marginally athletic? Or fathom that she could paralyze a six-foot tall young man in seconds with a formidable headlock?

Then again she was Mina Lin, a girl full of painfully pleasant surprises.

Grabbing Mina's arm, Jaiden locked her in place before spinning her around to face him. "Stop running away from me and just listen for a second," he pleaded.

The lack of expressions on her face annoyed him. He preferred seeing her smile or even frown. Not too long ago, he had realized how much he loved looking into her expressive brown eyes. Whenever he irked her, her cheeks glowed prettily pink. Whenever she was about to explode, she would scrunch her face up like a constipated child. Never had he seen her hide her emotions behind a poker face like now.

Heart pounding against his chest, he wondered if this was the best time to confess his feelings to her. It's now or never, he decided. Inhaling deeply, he mustered courage to speak the words of his heart. "I want you to be my girlfriend," he said with amplified sincerity in his tone. His violet-blue eyes darkened. "We don't have to pretend anymore." Squeezing Mina's hand, he hoped she could tell that he never wanted to let go of her. He stared at her lips, wanting to kiss her so badly but scared that she would push him away.

So he waited for her to respond. When she didn't, frustration swallowed him like flames devouring a building. *Why isn't she moved by my sincerity?* "Can't you tell that I like you?" Like a prepubescent boy, his voice cracked but he didn't care.

This is insane, he thought. What was it about Mina that made him so crazy about her?

Mina was still silent. Though she didn't say a word, her heartbeats thundered in her ears. If Jaiden could hear them, he would realize that she had feelings for him too.

Thoughts crowded in her head like hundreds of passengers in an Uptown train during rush hour. When he grimaced and looked at his injured shoulder, she hated herself for making him chase after her. A lot of time and physical therapy were needed for him to heal completely.

Maybe I should embrace and accept him. Do it, her heart told her.

But I don't decide with my heart. She looked down at her dirty sneakers, avoiding eye contact with Jaiden.

Jaiden winced from both pain and frustration. *Why isn't she looking at me?* He had a feeling that she wanted to run away again. His fingers wrapped around her hand tighter. "I don't just like you, Mina. I love you," he said with a quiver in his voice. He smiled, tears brimming in his beautiful eyes.

Mina swallowed a nonexistent lump in her throat. *He loves me?* She felt her heart swell with feeling. This feeling was strong and similar to what she had felt when she was still in love with Kiterin Forrests, the ex-boy-of-her-dreams.

She wanted to believe Jaiden. *Could it be true? He really loves me? But how? How could this be love?*

Mina peered at his face like a timid mouse, admiring his handsome features. His eyes were more midnight-violet than blue, reflecting his emotions. She wanted to run her finger along his straight nose and full lips. If Michelangelo were alive today, he would sculpt statues after Jaiden's likeness. *Adonis, move aside. David, wear some clothes.*

Everything Jaiden wore was expensive and exclusive to the affluent whereas Mina's entire wardrobe came from bargain bins. She still wore her dorky and linty clothes from her junior high school days. A son of a billionaire did not belong in her world. She and her recently reformed *gamble-holic* mother were part of the ninety-nine percent, whereas Jaiden and his father belonged to the point one percent.

So why say yes to Jaiden when Mina knew that he would inevitably break her heart? She shook her head. "How can you say you love me when we hardly know each other? Love doesn't work like that. Besides, your father hates me." She could see the veins bulging on his neck.

He did not expect such a response from her. He took a few seconds to digest her words. "What do you mean we hardly know each other?" He shook his head, seeming disappointed with her. "We've been through life and death together. And I don't care about what Father thinks. I love you. Isn't that enough?"

Mina wanted to say yes to Jaiden. In a fairytale world, love would be enough. She wanted to tell him that she loved him too. She questioned her feelings though. Was this love that she felt or was it purely gratitude? Was it just a silly crush?

All Mina knew was that in a short amount of time, Jaiden became someone special to her and secured a place in her heart.

Maybe we can be together, she thought briefly. She could be a damsel in distress and depend on Jaiden for financial support. She could say that she loved him too, date him, and then reap the benefits of being his girlfriend. Her life would be set, dazzling with glitz and glamour. She would lose herself in a dreamy world and forget about reality.

Falling from paradise would hurt more than glass shards impaling every layer of her skin. She had no doubt in her mind that one day he would dump her. After all, someone who could have anything and perhaps anyone in the world would quickly grow bored of someone like her. She wasn't hot enough. She wasn't special enough.

She wasn't Cinderella and this wasn't a fairy tale. Logically, she could never end up with a real life Prince Charming.

Despite being physically strong, Mina's heart was fragile like a butterfly. As easily as Jaiden could pluck the majestic insect's wings, he could shatter her heart.

"Now is just not the right time. We're too young." She shook her head again. "And I have so much to do and take care of... Mom, school, and college. I have to find a job and pay you back."

At first, Mina tried to convince herself that she had earned the fifty grand from Jaiden. After all, she had saved his life. Without needing to pay him back, she could cut all ties with him. She could focus on cleaning up the crap in her life and focus on building her future. But then her pride prevented her from keeping his money.

"Don't worry about the fifty grand... That money means nothing to me anyway." Because you mean everything to me, he wanted to add.

A few weeks ago, Jaiden easily helped pay off Mina's mother's fifty thousand dollar gambling debt with a single check. His nonchalance toward that crazy amount of money reminded Mina that they were from different worlds.

Mina pulled her hands away from Jaiden's. She turned to walk back to her house and forced herself not to cry. If Jaiden saw her crying, then he would know her heart disagreed with her actions and words. She looked at the sky, relying on gravity to keep her tears from escaping.

Jaiden sighed. "I don't care about the damn money!"

She turned around. "But I care. I just can't take your money even if it's insignificant to you."

"You deserved it. You saved my life."

"Anyone in my shoes would have done the same thing. Detective Graham did most of the work anyway." Which wasn't exactly true. Left to his own devices, that clumsy whiz-kid Graham would have found Jaiden dead, laying in a pool of his own blood in the middle of nowhere.

Jaiden rubbed his face in frustration. "I don't care about Graham or anyone else. I only care about you."

After taking a deep breath, Mina bit the insides of her lip. "Jaiden... I can't even think about starting a relationship with you now."

"Why not?" Jaiden looked at Mina like a confused puppy.

"Because we're from two different worlds," she said.

"Why does that matter?" Jaiden did not bother fighting back tears.

Mina felt the stings of a million wasps in her heart when she saw his tears. "It's... it's just that... I'm just not ready for a relationship." *I'm a coward. I don't want to face losing you one day. So I rather never be with you in the first place.*

"When will you be ready? When will the time be right for us?" he asked.

Mina wanted to take back her words, run toward him, and hug him so badly. But her answer was possibly never... "I don't know right now. I'm sorry, Jaiden. I'm sorry."

Jaiden watched her walk away. He felt as if someone with acid-dipped fingernails had just ripped out his still beating heart from his chest. So many women in his life had betrayed him. Barely five years old, he watched his mother walk away. In his mother's absence, Amelia, one of his maids, became the sole mother figure in his life. Jaiden grew to love Amelia. For years he had thought that she was really his mother. Thanks to Amelia, the hole his mother had created in his heart eventually healed.

Unfortunately for Jaiden, Amelia left him too when he was an adolescent. Never in his life had he felt more unloved and lonely. When he finally reunited with Amelia a few weeks ago, she came back to hurt him, playing a significant role in his kidnapping.

The ache in his heart increased the pain in his shoulder where Amelia had plunged a knife into. He remembered how much it had hurt. Surprisingly though, that flesh wound felt like a mosquito bite when compared to the heartbreak he felt now. If he didn't love Mina, then why did he shield her from Amelia's knife? He had risked his life for Mina and she repaid him with the coldness of an Ice Queen, cutting open his chest and slashing his heart to shreds. He wiped the tears off his face.

Why was she so cruel and complicated? He expected complication from socialites and gold diggers, but not from Mina. And since when did Jaiden have to beg anyone for anything? Girls always flocked to him like flies to honey and he always swatted them away. What was he to do now but walk away? He clenched his fists. "Fine. Just pretend I didn't say anything. I'm sorry for bothering you."

With her back against the front door, Mina forced herself not to cry. "Sorry, Jaiden..." She ran up to her room and watched him from her window.

Did I just throw away my happiness? She closed her eyes, hoping that her tears would stop flowing but a generous stream trickled down her cheeks.

Jaiden hoped that Mina would come out of her house. He waited for her but the minutes ticking away felt like hours. His pride killed his patience and forced him to walk away.

Don't look back. Don't think about her anymore. Jaiden convinced himself that he would forget about Mina Lin as long as he didn't see her again. Within time she would be but a memory to him. The pain in his broken heart would eventually be nothing but a whisper.

Or so he thought...

ABOUT THE AUTHOR

Kat Lieu is a Jackette-of-all-trades. By day, she's a physical therapist who has bare-handedly lifted 200-pound people with her impressive 5'2" frame. By night, she runs a tween/teen empire, Nummyz Productions. Nummyz Productions creates original Flash games for girls and provides them with a safe community, love advice, free stories, and support. Nummyz Productions publishes books and ebooks. Kat's company has also created websites for celebrities of The Young and the Restless and Flash games for multi-million dollar company LittleMissMatched.

For more information about Kat and her company, visit Nummyz.com. Follow Nummyz.com on Facebook and Twitter! Happy reading!

This book is dedicated to all my loved ones and the Maid for Me fans out there. Please make sure you leave me a review at Amazon.com! Send me a note! Poonpoonbom at gmail dot com. I can't wait to hear from you!